CLASSICS
Illustrated
Deluxe

WU CHENG'EN

THE MONKEY GOD

Adapted by Morvan,
Jian Yi, and Le Gal

PAPERCUTZ™

CLASSICS ILLUSTRATED DELUXE
GRAPHIC NOVELS FROM PAPERCUTZ

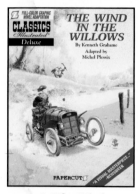

#1 "The Wind
In The Willows"

#2 "Tales From
The Brothers Grimm"

#3 "Frankenstein"

#4 "The Adventures
of Tom Sawyer"

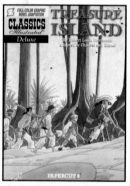

#5 "Treasure Island"

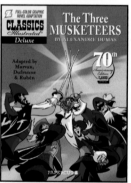

#6 "The Three Musketeers"

#7 "Around the World
in 80 Days"

#8 "Oliver Twist"

#9 Scrooge
"A Christmas Carol"
and "A Remembrance
of Mugby"

#10 "The Murders
in the Rue Morgue"
and Other Tales

#11 "The Sea-Wolf"

#12 "The Monkey God"

BY WU CHENG'EN

THE MONKEY GOD

Adapted by

Jean David Morvan
and Yann Le Gal
Script

Jian Yi
Art

CLASSICS
Illustrated®
Deluxe

#12

PAPERCUTZ™
New York

Thanks to Wang Peng for putting me in touch with Jian Yi, to Daisy and Philippe for warning me about his "concerns," to Captain Fab' for perilous settings, and to Yann Le Gal, who won't remain in the shadows very much longer! Thanks to the resident of Box104 for emigrating to the Beijing Hotel for a week—that's still going on.
J. D. M.

Thanks for everything to Jidi, my friend. Bravo to Jean-Louis for his incredible talent!
Y. L. G.

Here, I want to thank JD and Yann for the story writing, my friend Jingjin for the help of script translation and the comic artist Wang Peng for his instructions on my drawing, Lastly, I want to thank every reader who buys my book. They are the greatest encouragement to drive me to make drawings.
J. Y.

"The Monkey God"
By Wu Cheng'en
Adapted by
Jean David Morvan & Yann Le Gal - Writers
Jian Yi – Artist
Joe Johnson – Translation
Big Bird Zatryb – Lettering and Production
John Haufe and William B. Jones Jr. – Classics Illustrated Historians
Alexander Lu – Editorial Intern
Beth Scorzato – Production Coordinator
Michael Petranek – Editor
Jim Salicrup
Editor-in-Chief

ISBN: 978-1-62991-060-4 paperback edition
ISBN: 978-1-62991-061-1 hardcover edition

Papercutz books may be purchased for business or promotional use. For information on bulk purchases please contact Macmillan Corporate and Premium Sales Department at (800) 221-7945 x5442.

Printed in China
December 2014 by WKT Co. LTD
3/F Phase I Leader Industrial Centre
188 Texaco Road, Tseun Wan, N.T., Hong Kong

Distributed by Macmillan
First Papercutz Printing

Introduction

100!

That's the number of chapters that comprise the most famous of Chinese sagas: *Xiyouji*. The best-known version, attributed to Wu Cheng'en, was published in this form in the second half of the 16th Century. As strange as it might seem, this novel arises from a true story, that of a 17-year voyage undertaken by a Buddhist monk who went to India during the first half of the 7th Century. *Xuanzang*—that was his name—brought back from his trek a great number of Buddhist sutras, more than half of which he later translated, on the orders of the Emperor Taizong. The leader of the Tang Dynasty also ordered the traveler to supply him with the most precise description possible of the cultures he'd encountered. Terribly exotic for the era, these texts marked for centuries the collective imagination of the Chinese and, less than two hundred years after his demise, the life of *Xuanzang* had already entered into legend and become the subject of a popular tale in the form of a chantefable, mixing prose and poetry.

But from the historic reality to the novel, there is a gulf. For obviously, this monk never travelled in the company of a monkey seeking immortality, of a lazy pig capable of metamorphoses, and of a *bonze* (a Buddhist Monk) astride a demon prince transformed into a horse. All these characters will experience this *initiatory* quest in the hope of acquiring redemption therein.

Yes, this long tale is strongly tinged with the fantastic. The animals in it are endowed with speech and reason like humans, sometimes better even. In it, one crosses paths with dragons, witches, and monsters of every kind, which are more or less allegories of human behaviors that are easier to caricaturize under this form.

The Great Helmsman Mao Zedong saw himself in the monkey god–Sun Wukong being the incarnation of the revolutionary spirit that he imprinted on his country. All the studies conducted around this character by literary researchers in the course of the 20th Century are the basis of polemics concerning national identity, attesting therefore to the importance that this tale assumes in Chinese culture.

This novel is one of the four pillars of Chinese literature, along with *Water Margin*, *Dream of the Red Chamber*, and *The Romance of the Three Kingdoms*. Numerous representations of the tale's high points as well as of the main characters can be found in the form of drawings, frescoes, or bas-reliefs, attesting to their popularity in ancient times. Along with these three other masterpieces, it influenced the culture of other Asian countries, so much so that there exists very ancient editions of this text in Korea or in Japan, where one already finds a play version of *Xiyouji* as early as the 15th Century.

In Japan, there are numerous manga adaptations, from the most faithful to the most eccentric. A few examples include those of Osamu Tezuka (*The Legend of Songoku*, ed. Delcourt/Akata), and of Akira Toriyama (*Dragonball*). At the end of the 1970s, a televised series with 52 episodes was also produced, which was broadcast in nearly all of the countries of the world, with the exception of France. Let's not forget the recent musical by Damon Albarn and Jamie Hewlett, which was staged in Paris.

Xiyouji is already a perfectly paradoxical work, since it treads on serious matters in a playful manner. Within it, humor is omnipresent in form, and seriousness in content. But in the West, it gains another degree of paradox, since the public at large knows a few of its adaptations without ever being exposed to the original tale.

It's time to get back to the source!

– *Jean David Morvan*

PART ONE

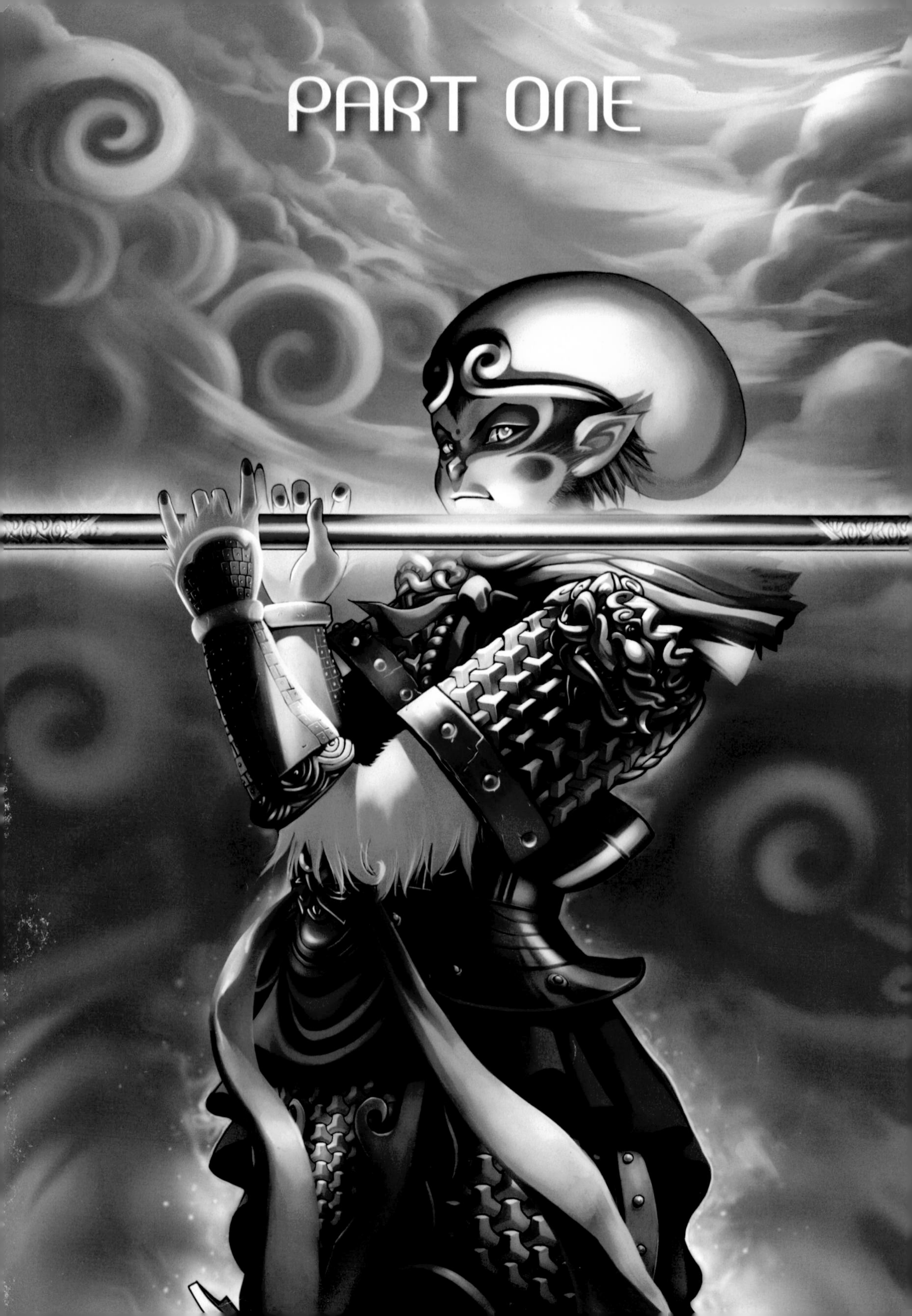

HIS NAME IS SUN WUKONG. HE'S THE KING OF MONKEYS. THE GREATEST OF HEROES!

FOR HIM, AS FOR US AND FOR ALL THOSE WHO LIVE ON EARTH, A DAY IS DIVIDED THUSLY:

THE SOLAR INFLUX RISES AT THE HOUR OF THE RAT.

THE COCK CROWS AT THE HOUR OF THE OX.

THE LIGHT HIDES WHEN THAT OF THE TIGER ARRIVES.

THE SUN APPEARS AT THAT OF THE HARE.

AFTER LUNCH COMES THE HOUR OF THE DRAGON.

THE SUN IS AT IT'S ZENITH AT THE HOUR OF THE HORSE.

AT THAT OF THE GOAT, THE SUN GOES BACK DOWN.

WE EAT AT THAT OF THE MONKEY.

THE SUN SETS AT THE HOUR OF THE ROOSTER.

TWILIGHT MARKS THAT OF THE DOG.

FINALLY, REST COMES AT THE HOUR OF THE PIG.

IT IS THE SAME FOR THE UNIVERSE, OF WHICH A CYCLE MEASURES ONE HUNDRED TWENTY-NINE THOUSAND SIX HUNDRED YEARS. EXCEPT THAT ITS PHASES ARE OF TEN THOUSAND EIGHT HUNDRED YEARS.

DARKNESS AT THE DOG...

...CHAOS AT THE PIG...

THE HEAVENS OPENED AT THE RAT.

AT THE BEGINNING OF THE OX, CERTAIN ELEMENTS BEGAN TO SOLIDIFY...

...AND AT ITS COMPLETION, FORMED WATER, FIRE, MOUNTAINS, ROCKS, AND EARTH, WHICH ARE CALLED THE FIVE FORMS.

FINALLY, CAME THE PHASE OF THE TIGER, IN WHICH THE FEMALE YIN AND THE MALE YANG UNITED TO GIVE RISE TO ALL LIVING CREATURES.

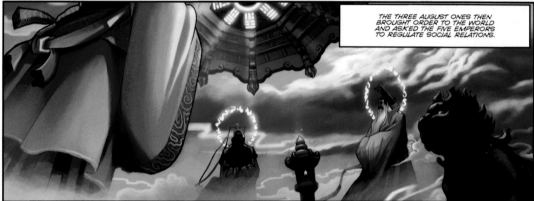

THE THREE AUGUST ONES THEN BROUGHT ORDER TO THE WORLD, AND ASKED THE FIVE EMPERORS TO REGULATE SOCIAL RELATIONS.

THE FOUR GREAT CONTINENTS WERE DEFINED, TO THE NORTH, THE SOUTH, THE WEST...

...AND TO THE EAST, WHICH IS WHAT THIS STORY WILL CONCERN.

IT BEGINS IN THE LAND OF ALOAI, MORE PRECISELY ON THE MOUNTAIN OF FLOWERS AND FRUIT.

ON ITS SUMMIT SAT THIS IMMORTAL ROCK.

EVER SINCE THE WORLD HAD
ITS NAME, THIS MOUNTAIN
HAD BEEN SHAPED BY THE
PURITIES OF HEAVEN...

...AND EARTHLY LUXURIANCE.

CARESSED BY THE VIGOR
OF SUNBEAMS...

...AND THE
SOFTNESS OF
MOONBEAMS.

IT'S THROUGH
THESE PARADOXES
THAT IT BECAME
PREGNANT...

...AND BROUGHT
FORTH A STONE
EGG ABOUT THE
SIZE OF A BALL.

THE LATTER WAS
SHAPED BY A
STORM-SAGE,
WHO GAVE TO IT
FIVE SENSES AND
FOUR LIMBS.

THUS DID SUN WUK'ONG COME INTO THE WORLD. WE SHALL RECOUNT HIS EXTRAORDINARY ADVENTURES TO YOU, AND HOW HE BECAME IMMORTAL... AT THE END OF HIS EVENTFUL PILGRIMAGE INTO THE WEST.

INSTINCTIVELY, HE LEARNED TO STAND UPRIGHT...

...AND CLIMBED ONTO HIS MOTHER EARTH'S SHOULDERS.

HIGH UP AND WELL PERCHED, HE HAILED THE 4 QUARTERS, WHICH WERE SOLIDLY ATTACHED TO HIS PROGENITRIX.

BEFORE PAYING HOMAGE TO HIS FATHER HEAVEN.

THAT'S WHEN FROM HIS GAZE TWO GOLDEN BEAMS SHONE FORTH.

AT THE SPEED OF LIGHT, THEY PIERCED THE CLOUDS THAT SERVE AS FOUNDATIONS FOR THE PALACE OF THE SOLAR STAR.

!?

TRAVERSING THE DOWNY FLOOR OF THE TREASURE ROOM OF THE MYSTERIOUS MISTS, THEY STARTLED THE JADE EMPEROR.

IN THE PRESENCE OF HIS MINISTERS, THE GREAT COMPASSIONATE ONE OF THE HIGHEST HEAVENLY SPHERES CALLED FOR HIS HERALDS.

THOUSAND-MILE EYE!

THOUSAND-MILE WIND!

TAKE THE SOUTHERN CELESTIAL DOOR TO DISCOVER WHENCE THOSE RAYS CAME.

WE OBEY!

I SEE TRACES OF MOVEMENT!

INDEED, I SENSE SOMETHING OVER THAT WAY!

IT'S NO DOUBT COMING FROM HIM!

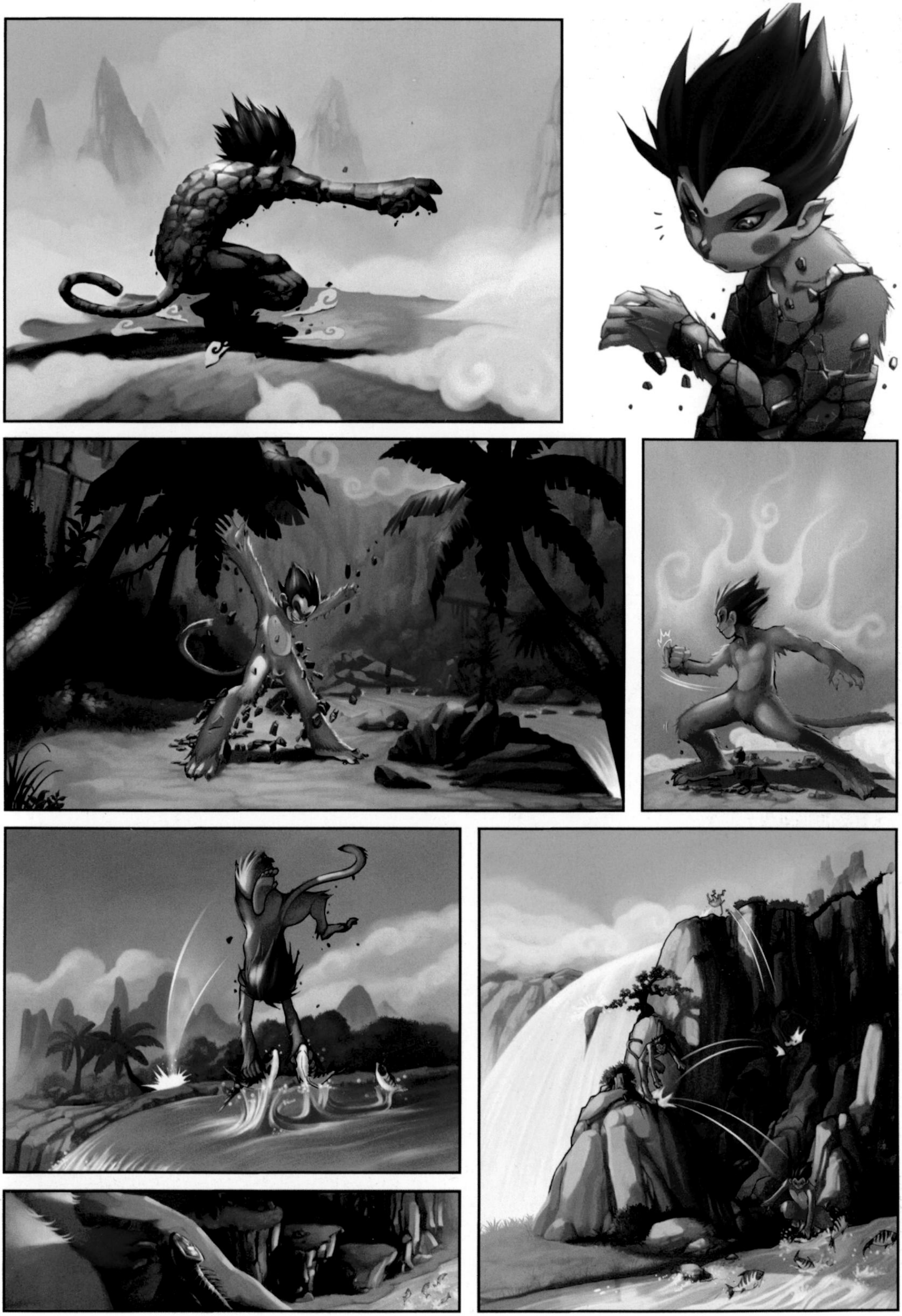

THUS SATED, THE APE-LIKE
GROUP ACCEPTED HIS PRESENCE.

HE LIVED WITH THEM AT THE EDGE OF THE SMALL LAND OF THE HERALDS, TO THE EAST OF THE SEA OF THE EASTERN CONTINENT.

THE RADIANCE OF HIS EYES HAD DIMMED SINCE HE NOW SWALLOWS FOOD AND WATER.

BAH, THERE'S NOTHING SPECIAL ABOUT BEINGS LIVING UNDER OUR FEET.

THIS ONE, HOWEVER, ISN'T EXACTLY LIKE THE OTHERS. CERTAINLY, HE CAN WALK, RUN, LEAP, TELL GOOD BERRIES FROM BAD, LIKE ALL MONKEYS.

BUT WHAT'S MORE, HE HAS THE ABILITY TO COME TO AGREEMENTS WITH SAVAGE BEASTS SUCH AS THE PANTHERS OR TIGERS, TO GET ALONG WITH THE BUCKS OR DOES-- OR ALSO TO BECOME INFATUATED WITH ALL THE RACES THAT COMPOSE HIS SPECIES.

IN SHORT, HE REASONS.

HMM, TELL ME MORE THEN.

AND IT WAS BY USING HIS MIND THAT HE BECAME KING.

ONE DAY, THE MONKEYS WONDERED WHENCE CAME THE WATER THAT CREATED THE LAKE WHERE THEY'D ESTABLISHED THEIR HOMES, BEFORE FLOWING INTO THE OCEAN.

SO THEY WENT UPSTREAM TO THE TOP OF THE MOUNTAIN, TO THE SOURCE, WHICH PROVED TO BE THE MOST MAGNIFICENT OF WATERFALLS.

ALL TOGETHER, THEY PLEDGED TO BECOME THE FAITHFUL SUBJECTS OF WHOEVER WOULD BE CLEVER ENOUGH TO GO THROUGH THE FALL AND COME OUT IN ONE PIECE.

IT'S AT THAT MOMENT, EXTRICATING HIMSELF FROM THE GROUP AND CLOSING HIS EYES, THAT HE WHOM THEY'D DUBBED "STONE MONKEY" SEALED HIS FATE...

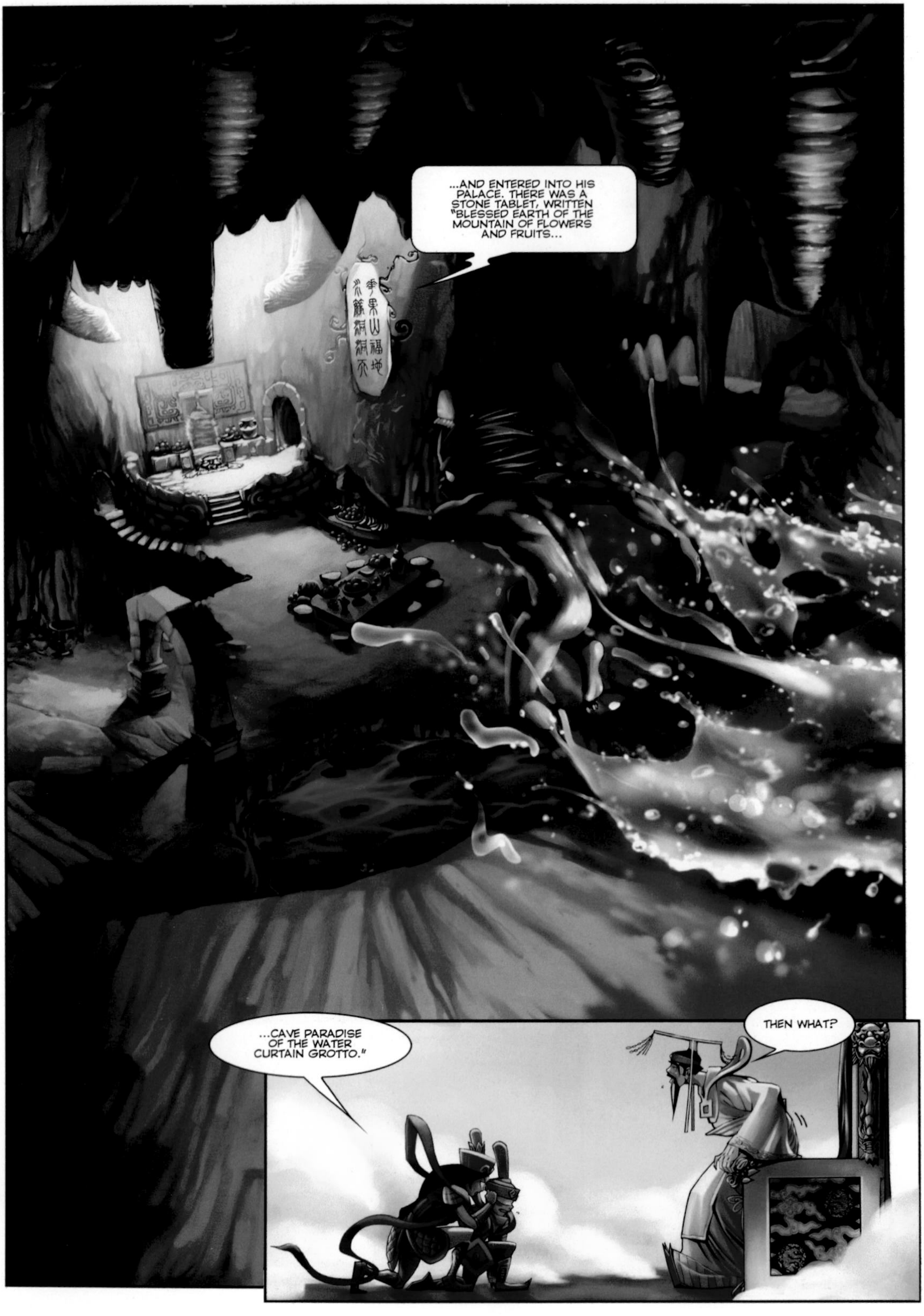
...AND ENTERED INTO HIS PALACE. THERE WAS A STONE TABLET, WRITTEN "BLESSED EARTH OF THE MOUNTAIN OF FLOWERS AND FRUITS...
...CAVE PARADISE OF THE WATER CURTAIN GROTTO."
THEN WHAT?

AFTER BRINGING HIS COMRADES IN, I FOLLOWED ALONG AS BEST I MIGHT, BUT COULD ONLY SEE POORLY THROUGH THE CURTAIN OF WATER.

FEAR NOT AND LISTEN TO ME!

AND THE ROAR OF THE WATER COVERED A GOOD PORTION OF HIS WORDS, BUT I THOUGHT I UNDERSTOOD THAT HE GAVE THEM A SPEECH.

NEVERMORE WILL THE WIND ASSAULT US, NOR THE RAIN DRENCH US. AN END TO THE ANGUISH OF THE ARRIVAL OF STORMS, SNOWS, AND OTHER FROSTS. HERE WE ARE FINALLY SHELTERED FROM NATURE'S TORMENTS.

HERE, WE ARE AT HOME!

LONG LIVE OUR GREAT KING! LONG LIVE OUR GREAT KING!

HENCEFORTH, "STONE MONKEY" HAS DISAPPEARED, REPLACED BY...

THE HANDSOME MONKEY KING.

CLEARLY, THIS PRIMATE IS OUT OF THE ORDINARY.

AND THAT WAS ONLY THE BEGINNING OF OUR SURVEILLANCE.

HE NEXT NAMED VARIOUS MACAQUES AND GIBBONS AS MINISTERS OR SERVANTS.

THEN HE LIVED IT UP FOR A LONG WHILE, BUT I COULD HEAR IN THE SOUND OF HIS VOICE THAT SOMETHING WAS TROUBLING HIM.

IT WAS DURING A BANQUET OF 10,000 FRUITS THAT HE BURST INTO TEARS.

HIS SUBJECTS, WORRIED, INQUIRED ABOUT HIS SUFFERING.

O HANDSOME MONKEY KING, WHAT TROUBLES YOU?

AH, IT IS BECAUSE I CANNOT KEEP MYSELF FROM THINKING ABOUT THE FUTURE. ABOUT THE MOMENT WHEN LIFE WILL CEASE FOR ME.

WHEN OLD AND DECREPIT, MY SOUL WILL BE TAKEN TO THE KINGDOM OF SHADOWS, DIRECTED BY DEATH'S IRON HAND.

CAN I BE PROUD OF HAVING LIVED IF I CANNOT REMAIN ETERNALLY AMONG THE DIVINE BEINGS?

THAT'S WHEN THE MOST LEARNED OF HIS COUNCILORS TOOK THE FLOOR.

DO YOU KNOW THAT BUT THREE KINDS OF BEINGS ELUDE THE KING OF HELL?

THEY ARE THE BUDDHAS, THE IMMORTALS, AND THE SAGES. THEY WILL FOREVER BE THE AGE OF THE UNIVERSE.

AND WHERE DO THEY LIVE?

IN OUR WORLD, IN ANCIENT CAVES AND AMID AGELESS MOUNTAINS.

THEN, STARTING AT DAWN, CUT ME ENOUGH WOOD TO MAKE A RAFT! MAKE PLANS FOR A LONG POLE AND PROVISIONS, TOO.

TOMORROW, EVEN IF I MUST GO TO THE ENDS OF THE EARTH OR SEA, I SHALL FIND ONE OF THOSE THREE.

AND I SWEAR HE'LL TEACH ME TO LIVE FOREVER!

IN THE MORNING, WE WATCHED HIM SET HIS RAFT UPON THE WATER AND CLIMB ABOARD.

NOT WISHING TO WAIT FOR CHANCE TO BRING HIM TO HIS DESTINATION, WE ASCENDED ABOVE THE CLOUDS TO REQUEST A LITTLE ASSISTANCE.

HO PO, THE GOD OF THE YELLOW RIVER, POURED MORE WATER INTO THE SEA TO ACCELERATE THE FLOW OF THE MOUNTAIN BROOKS.

AND CHI PO HASTENED THE WINDS OF WHICH HE WAS THE MASTER, ONCE THE RAFT WAS ON THE OCEAN.

AS FOR MAZU, SHE PROTECTED OUR SAILOR, AND THANKS TO THE CURRENTS, HAD HIM REACH THE NORTHWESTERN COAST OF THE SOUTHERN CONTINENT FASTER THAN NORMAL.

HE CAME ASHORE AT A HAMLET OF FISHERMEN.

HE NOTICED THEIR FRIGHTENED FACES AND YELLED, SCARING THE COWARDLY VILLAGERS AWAY.

HE KNOCKED ONE OF THE VILLAGERS OUT, MORE OR LESS OF HIS SIZE, AND TOOK HIS CLOTHING.

SEEING HOW THEY WELCOMED STRANGERS...

...HE UNDERSTOOD THAT HE WOULD HAVE TO BE DISCREET ABOUT HIS VOYAGE TOWARDS IMMORTALITY.

THEN BY WANDERING THE TOWNS AND VILLAGES OF THE SOUTHERN CONTINENT, HE OBSERVED HUMAN BEHAVIOR, APING THEM TO PERFECTION.

EIGHT OR NINE YEARS LATER, WHEN HE WAS CROSSING A FOREST THAT SERVED AS A FLOOR MAT TO A MAJESTIC MOUNTAIN...

I CHOP TREES, BOTH BIG AND SMALL,

IN BUNDLES, TO SELL THEM ALL.

A HORRIBLY BELLOWED SONG PIERCED HIS EARDRUMS.

TOWN TO TOWN, TILL SALE'S COMPLETE, WANDER FAR FOR RICE TO EAT.

THUS MY LIFE GOES BY, I SWEAR, MEETING OFT IMMORTALS THERE.

AH, SO THERE ARE IMMORTALS HEREABOUTS?

SEATED, NEVER WITHOUT VOICE, IN THE YELLOW COURT THEY REJOICE.

GOOD DAY, VENERABLE IMMORTAL!

KNOW THAT I WILL BE THE MOST ATTENTIVE OF STUDENTS.

...

AH, YOU'RE CONFUSED, LITTLE HAIRY MAN. I, ALAS, AM NAUGHT BUT PERISHABLE MEAT.

THE YELLOW COURT CONTAINS MANY TRUTHFUL WORDS ABOUT THE WAY AND VIRTUE, DOESN'T IT?

AH, I UNDERSTAND...

I AM NOT AN IMMORTAL, BUT THE NEIGHBOR WHO TAUGHT ME THAT SONG IS ONE.

TELL ME QUICK WHERE TO FIND HIM!

SEE THAT MOUNTAIN? ITS NAME IS "MOUNTAIN OF THE GODS' TERRACE OF A SQUARE THUMB." IT'S ALSO CALLED: "THE HEART."

THERE YOU WILL DISCOVER THE CAVE OF THE SLANTING MOON AND THREE STARS IN WHICH LIVES THE IMMORTAL SUBHUTI.

AT PRESENT, HE'S EDUCATING SOME THIRTY STUDENTS IN THE WAY.

MY THANKS TO YOU, WISE CRAFTSMAN!

OPEN! OPEN TO THE MONKEY KING!

ARE THEY DEAF IN THERE, OR WHAT?

IS THAT YOU MAKING SUCH A RACKET?!

IMMORTAL CHILD, AS A DISCIPLE IN THE WAY AND OF IMMORTALITY, NEVER WOULD I DARE MAKE THE SLIGHTEST RACKET IN THIS PLACE.

AH, SO IT IS YOUR PRESENCE THAT MY MASTER DIVINED UPON AWAKENING, AND WHOM HE ASKED ME TO GO GREET.

OF COURSE IT'S ME! WHO ELSE?!

THEN, FOLLOW ME.

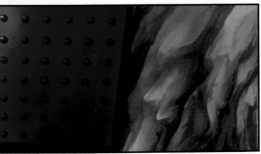

THROW THAT IMPOSTOR OUT FOR ME!

BUT I SWEAR TO YOU I DO COME FROM THE EASTERN CONTINENT...

THAT'S IMPOSSIBLE. THERE ARE TWO OCEANS AND ANOTHER ENTIRE CONTINENT BETWEEN HERE AND THERE!

I TRAVELLED FOR 10 YEARS. AND AS MY PARENTS ARE THE PRIMORDIAL ELEMENTS, THEY PROTECTED ME.

INTERESTING.

AND WHAT ABOUT YOUR NAME?

NO ONE EVER GAVE ME ONE.

THEN I SHALL DO SO. WHAT DO YOU THINK OF "CONSCIOUS OF EMPTINESS"?

SUN WUKONG!

THAT'S EXACTLY WHAT I EXPECTED WITHOUT KNOWING IT.

IT IS NECESSARY TO NAME CHAOS IN ORDER TO END ITS REIGN.

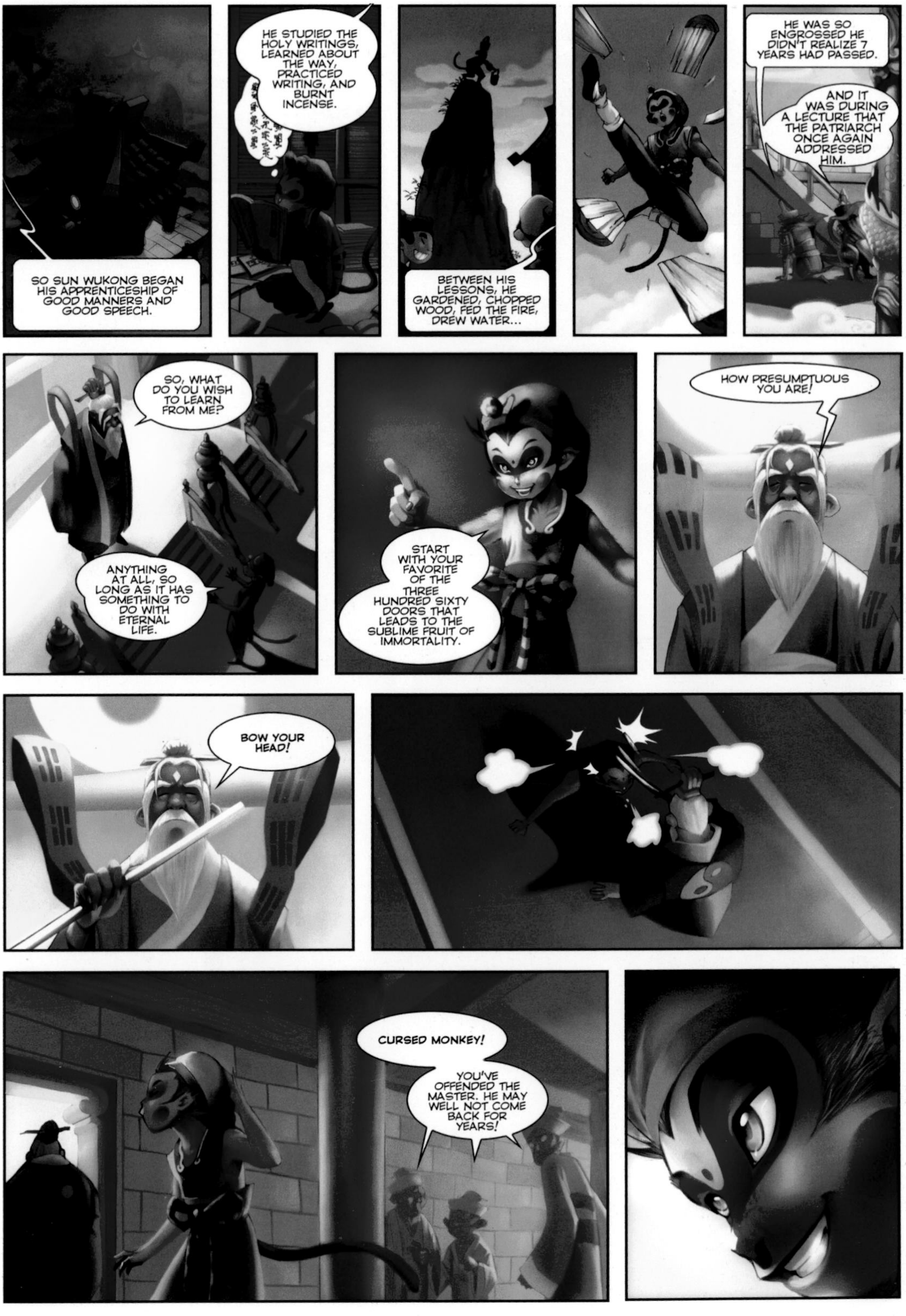
SO SUN WUKONG BEGAN HIS APPRENTICESHIP OF GOOD MANNERS AND GOOD SPEECH.
HE STUDIED THE HOLY WRITINGS, LEARNED ABOUT THE WAY, PRACTICED WRITING, AND BURNT INCENSE.
BETWEEN HIS LESSONS, HE GARDENED, CHOPPED WOOD, FED THE FIRE, DREW WATER...
HE WAS SO ENGROSSED HE DIDN'T REALIZE 7 YEARS HAD PASSED.
AND IT WAS DURING A LECTURE THAT THE PATRIARCH ONCE AGAIN ADDRESSED HIM.
SO, WHAT DO YOU WISH TO LEARN FROM ME?
ANYTHING AT ALL, SO LONG AS IT HAS SOMETHING TO DO WITH ETERNAL LIFE.
START WITH YOUR FAVORITE OF THE THREE HUNDRED SIXTY DOORS THAT LEADS TO THE SUBLIME FRUIT OF IMMORTALITY.
HOW PRESUMPTUOUS YOU ARE!
BOW YOUR HEAD!
CURSED MONKEY!
YOU'VE OFFENDED THE MASTER. HE MAY WELL NOT COME BACK FOR YEARS!

WHY AREN'T YOU SLEEPING WITH YOUR FELLOW DISCIPLES, CURSED MONKEY?

COME NOW, MASTER, YOU SIGNALED TO ME TO COME JOIN YOU.

INDEED NOW-- AND IN WHAT TERMS?

YOU STRUCK ME THREE TIMES ON THE HEAD, THEN LEFT BEHIND MY BACK, CLOSING THE CENTRAL DOOR.

IT SEEMED OBVIOUS TO ME YOU WERE SUMMONING ME TO YOUR APARTMENTS.

AT THE THIRD WATCH OF THE NIGHT, BY PASSING THROUGH THE REAR DOOR.

YOU'RE AS CLEVER AS THE REST OF YOUR KIND...

NOBODY HAS EVER DECODED MY HIDDEN SIGNS. IT IS TO YOU, THEREFORE, THAT I WILL TEACH THE ADMIRABLE WAY TO ENDLESS LIFE.

I'LL LISTEN TO YOU LIKE NEVER BEFORE.

IN ORDER TO PENETRATE IN FULLNESS THIS HITHERTO UNHEARD-OF SECRET, YOU WILL NEED TO CULTIVATE AN ENERGY LIKE NO OTHER.

AND HE RECITED TO HIM A WHOLE TEXT TOO LONG AND COMPLICATED FOR ME TO RETAIN IT.

IT'S USELESS FOR YOU TO KNOW IT; IN ANY CASE, SINCE YOU'RE IMMORTAL.

CERTAINLY. AND HE WAS "CONSCIOUSNESS OF EMPTINESS" THEN?

HE SPENT 3 YEARS CONSOLIDATING HIS KNOWLEDGE OF RADICAL ORIGIN.

INDEED. GET TO THE FACTS.

WELL, IN TIME, WUKONG BECAME AN EXPERT IN THE ART OF 72 TRANSFORMATIONS.

AND HAD LEARNED TO RIDE ASTRIDE THE CLOUDS.

THE ONLY THING THAT THE SAGE SUBHŪTI HADN'T SUCCEEDED IN TEACHING HIM WAS HOW TO AVOID THE THREE CALAMITIES THAT WOULD BEFALL HIM AT 500 YEAR INTERVALS.

THAT OF LIGHTNING...

...THAT OF THE INTERNAL FIRE...

...AND THAT OF WIND BLOWING AWAY BONES AND FLESH.

YES, I KNOW. I'M THE ONE WHO IS SUPPOSED TO SUBJECT HIM TO THESE TRIALS FOR HAVING VIOLATED THE MYSTERY OF THE SUN AND MOON.

SUBHŪTI DIDN'T TEACH WUKONG HOW TO AVOID THE CALAMITIES BECAUSE HE'S NOT HUMAN, RIGHT?

EXACTLY.

IN ANY CASE, LATER ON, HE WAS SENT BACK TO HIS HOME.

AND CAN YOU DO THIS?

HE WAS SO PROUD OF TURNING INTO A PINE TREE THAT HIS BOISTEROUS BELLOWS ALMOST BURST MY EARDRUMS!

WUKONG, YOU DISAPPOINT ME BY USING YOUR POWERS TO AMUSE OTHERS.

GO HOME NOW, YOU HAVE NOTHING FURTHER TO LEARN HERE. AND IF YOU CAUSE THE SLIGHTEST CATASTROPHE, I FORBID YOU TO CALL YOURSELF MY DISCIPLE.

OTHERWISE, I'LL CRUSH YOU, BODY AND SOUL.

IF YOU DID SO, IT'D BE BECAUSE I DESERVED IT, AND I'D ACCEPT YOUR PUNISHMENT GRACIOUSLY.

THANK YOU FOR EVERYTHING, O WISE SUBHUTI.

SO SUN WUKONG SLIPPED ALONG THE CURRENTS BACK TO HIS HOME, THE MOUNTAIN OF FRUITS AND FLOWERS.

AND HE DISCOVERED A VERY SAD SPECTACLE THERE.

...

IT'S REALLY HIM! HE'S BACK!

O GREAT KING, WE WERE AFRAID YOU'D ABANDONED US FOR ETERNITY.

NOT ON YOUR LIFE! BUT WHO'S RESPONSIBLE FOR THIS HORROR?

THE DEMON OF CHAOS WHO RESIDES IN THE NORTH. HE WANTS TO LIVE IN OUR CAVE!

WE'RE CONDUCTING A HOPELESS BATTLE AGAINST HIM. HE IS RUTHLESS!

CORRECTION: HE WAS RUTHLESS.

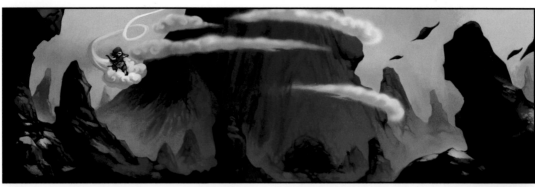

OUR GOOD KING! THANK YOU FOR SAVING US!

FROM NOW ON, NO ONE WILL HARM YOU!

WHO ARE YOU, TINY THIEF?

THE WORLD WILL REMEMBER ME BY THE NAME OF SUN WUKONG, "CONSCIOUS OF EMPTINESS!"

"CONSCIOUS OF BEING SLICED IN TWO" WOULD SUIT YOU BETTER!

WHERE ARE YOU, LITTLE MORSEL?! I'M GOING TO DEVOUR YOU!

?

AH, BUT YOU WOULDN'T WANT TO RISK ME GETTING STUCK IN YOUR THROAT!

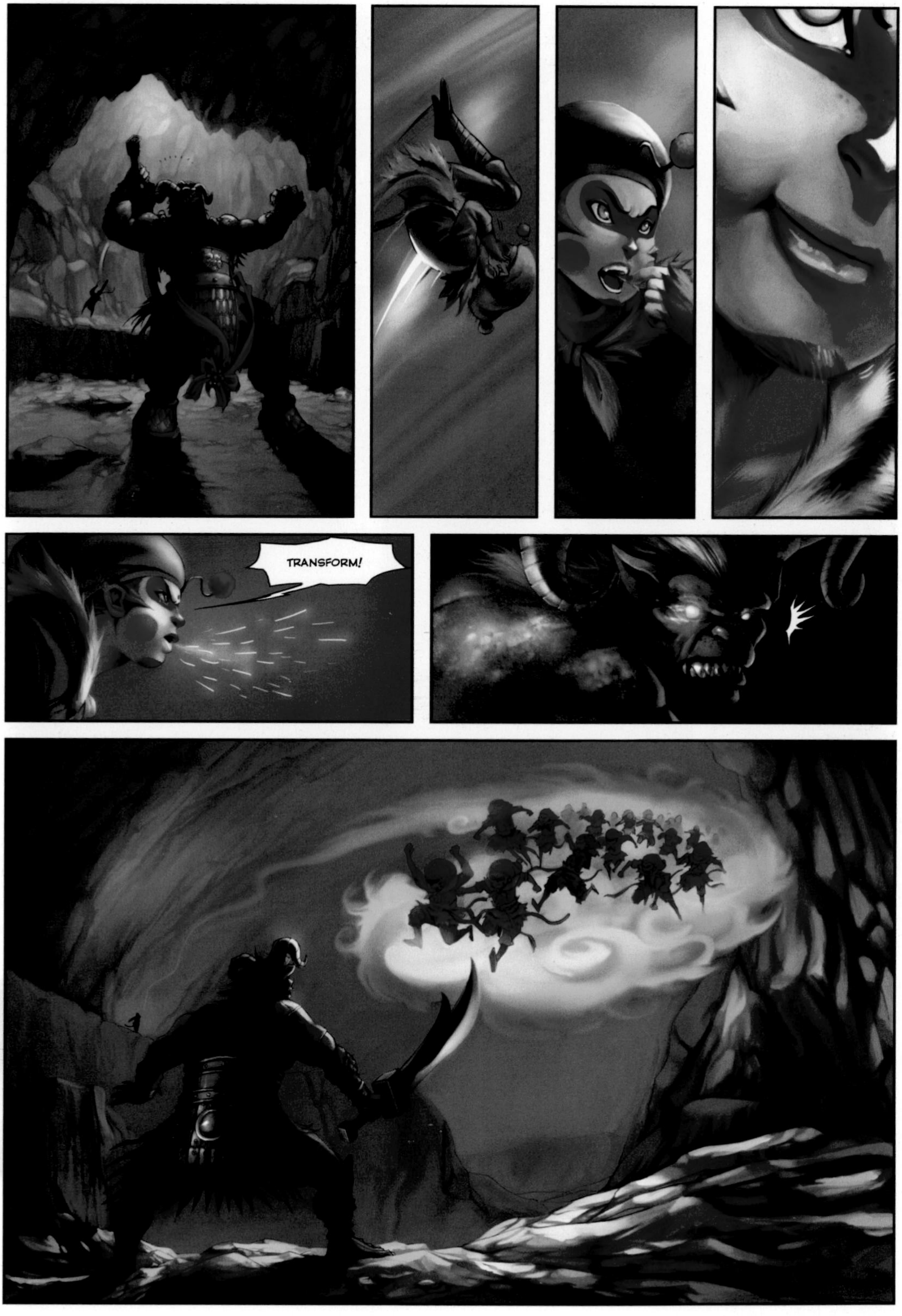
TRANSFORM!

ALRIGHT,
WE'RE GOING
HOME.

AND DID HE SETTLE DOWN A LITTLE AFTERWARDS?

IN A SENSE. HE SPENT YEARS TRAINING HIMSELF IN THE MARTIAL ARTS USING THE GREAT SABER HE'D WON.

AND AS HE WAS BORED TRAINING BY HIMSELF, HE HAD TREES CUT INTO THE SHAPE OF SABERS FOR HIS FELLOW MONKEYS.

TOGETHER, THEY LEARNED TO EXECUTE WONDROUS WARLIKE ROUTINES.

BUT ONE DAY, A PERFECTLY PARADOXICAL IDEA TOOK ROOT IN SUN WUKONG'S HEAD...

MY FRIENDS, LISTEN TO ME ONE MOMENT...

YOU HAVE BECOME SO ADEPT IN THE HANDLING OF WOODEN WEAPONS...

...THAT YOU MIGHT FRIGHTEN SOME KING OF MEN, ANIMALS OR FOWL.

IF ANOTHER KING BEGAN TO THINK WE WERE PREPARING FOR WAR, HE WOULD IMMEDIATELY ATTACK US.

AND WITH WOODEN WEAPONS, WE'D HAVE NO CHANCE OF OFFERING HIM ANY REAL RESISTANCE.

TRULY, WE NEED BLADES THAT SLICE AND AXES THAT SMASH...

O GREAT KING, "CONSCIOUS OF EMPTINESS," DO WE RIGHTLY UNDERSTAND WHAT YOU SAID?

ARE YOU IN SEARCH OF METAL WEAPONS? DID YOU KNOW THAT A MAGNIFICENT CITY PROSPERS TO THE EAST OF OUR MOUNTAINS?

ITS KING, SOLDIERS, AND INHABITANTS ENJOY THE USE OF TOOLS MADE FROM GOLD, SILVER, COPPER, BRONZE, IRON, AND OTHER VARIOUS METALS.

PERHAPS YOU COULD GO THERE AND ORDER THE CRAFTSMEN TO MAKE WEAPONS FOR YOU.

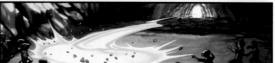

HMM, WHY SHOULD I WAIT FOR WEAPONS TO BE FASHIONED FOR ME WHEN THERE ARE SURELY ALL MANNER OF FULLY FORGED WEAPONS IN THE PALACE ARSENAL?

AFTER ALL, THEY'RE WITHIN REACH OF ONLY ONE SIMPLE, LITTLE SPELL.

AHA, A TORNADO, BUT TO WHAT END?

THE FRIGHTENED FOLK SOUGHT SHELTER IN THEIR HOMES.

AND SUN WUKONG HAD FREE REIN IN THE ARSENAL.

THERE'S EVEN MORE THAN I COULD HAVE DREAMT OF IN HERE.

...BUT I ONLY HAVE TWO ARMS, AND I'D REALLY NEED A THOUSAND MORE TO TRANSPORT EVERYTHING.

I GOT IT!

THIS IS NO GOOD.

I SEE YOU ALL BEFORE ME, SATISFIED WITH YOUR WEAPONS.

AND I'M HAPPY FOR YOU.

BUT I MUST ADMIT TO YOU THAT I DON'T LIKE MY SWORD ANY LONGER. IT'S TOO CUMBERSOME AND NOT ATTRACTIVE.

O OUR KING, THAT'S QUITE TO BE EXPECTED. YOUR IMMORTAL NATURE MAKES YOU ILL-SUITED TO COMMON WEAPONS.

WE MAY HAVE A SOLUTION FOR YOU, BUT WE'RE UNSURE IF YOU'RE CAPABLE OF BREATHING UNDER WATER.

LET'S BE SERIOUS. DON'T FORGET THAT THE WAY WAS REVEALED TO ME.

THE SEVENTY-TWO TRANSFORMATIONS I HAVE MASTERED ALLOW ME TO LIVE WHEREVER I LIKE.

IN THAT CASE, MAYBE YOU COULD VISIT THE OLD DRAGON.

HE REIGNS IN THE DEPTHS OF THE EASTERN SEA.

BEING OF THE SAME RANK, PERHAPS YOU TWO COULD CONVERSE TOGETHER.

THEN, HE'LL GIFT YOU WITH A WEAPON TO YOUR LIKING.

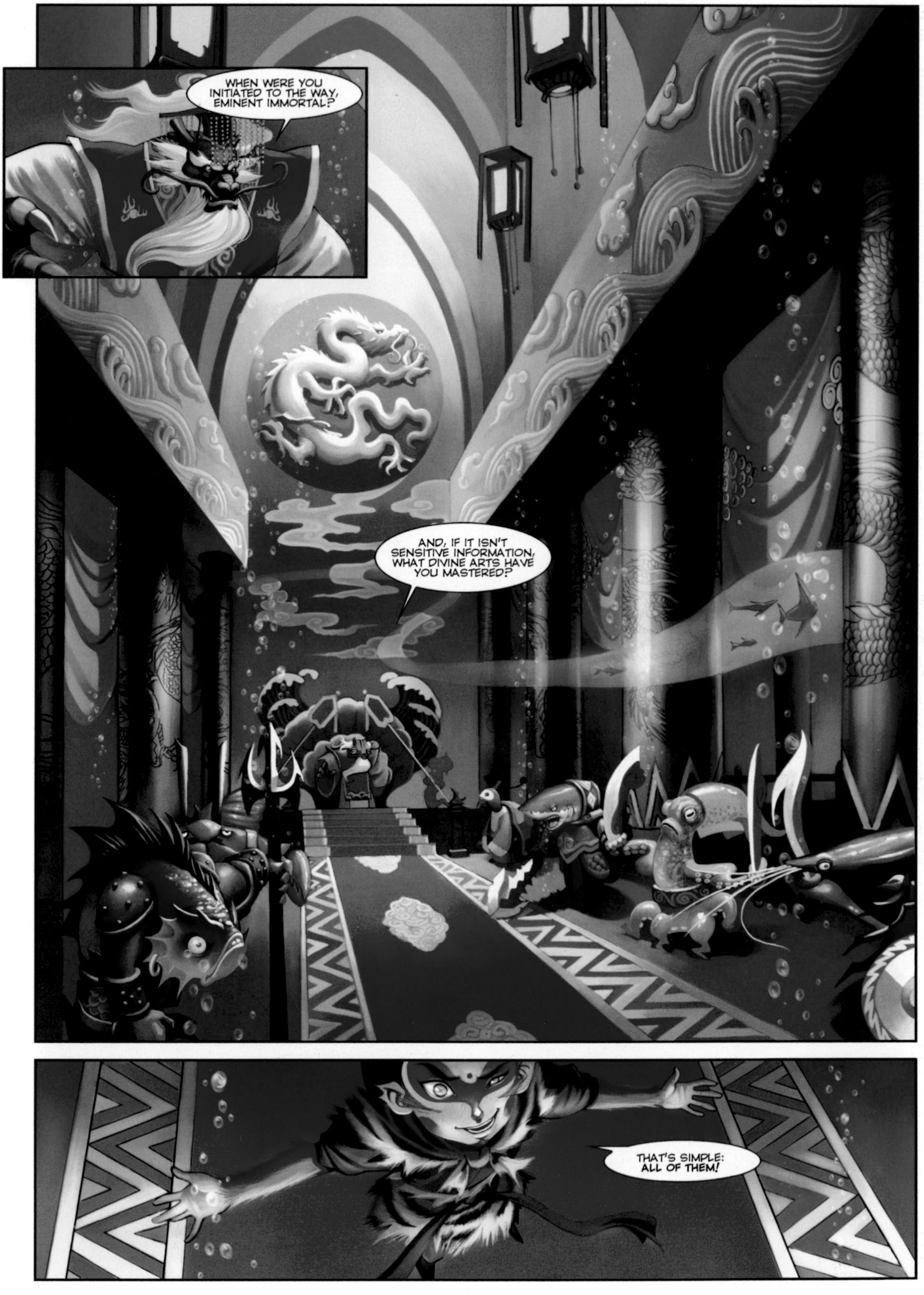
WHEN WERE YOU INITIATED TO THE WAY, EMINENT IMMORTAL?
AND, IF IT ISN'T SENSITIVE INFORMATION, WHAT DIVINE ARTS HAVE YOU MASTERED?
THAT'S SIMPLE: ALL OF THEM!

I DIDN'T COME, HOWEVER, TO SPEAK OF THAT.

I WANTED TO PROTECT THE APPROACHES TO MY KINGDOM IN THE MOUNTAIN...

...BUT THEN I REALIZED I DIDN'T HAVE A SUITABLE WEAPON.

OVER THE YEARS, I HAVE HEARD MUCH GOOD SPOKEN OF YOU, MY WISE AND POWERFUL NEIGHBOR WHOM INHABITS A JASPER PALACE WITH A MOTHER-OF-PEARL DOORWAY.

I TOLD MYSELF I'D COME SPEAK TO YOU OF MY PROBLEM.

FOR YOUR REPUTATION SAYS THAT YOU ENJOY THE USE OF A GREAT EXCESS OF DIVINE WEAPONS.

PERHAPS YOU WOULD LET ME CHOOSE ONE OF THEM.

HOW COULD I REFUSE SUCH A SMALL FAVOR TO SO POWERFUL AN EQUAL?

SERVANTS, GO IMMEDIATELY AND FIND WHAT OUR VENERABLE NEIGHBOR HAS DEMANDED!

NO, NO, AND NO! IT'S TOO LIGHT. IT DOESN'T SUIT ME.

FIND ME SOMETHING ELSE!

BUT UNSURPASSED IMMORTAL, YOU HAVE JUST TRIED ALL THE WEAPONS I POSSESS, AND THAT ONE IS THE HEAVIEST! I HAVE NOTHING FURTHER TO OFFER YOU!

MAJESTIC FATHER, YOU SHOULD PRESENT WUKONG WITH THAT MARVELOUS MAGIC STAFF WHICH YU THE GREAT USED TO MEASURE THE STARS AND THE DEPTHS OF THE OCEANS.

A MAGIC STAFF? BRING IT TO ME RIGHT AWAY!

ALAS, IT'S TOO BIG AND TOO HEAVY! WE CANNOT TRANSPORT IT.

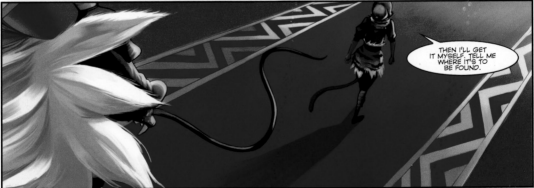

THEN I'LL GET IT MYSELF. TELL ME WHERE IT'S TO BE FOUND.

EXTRAORDINARY! I MUST HAVE IT!

BUT IT'S A LITTLE TOO BIG TO CARRY IT HOME.

BUT WITH A SIMPLE, LITTLE SPELL...

I THANK YOU SINCERELY FOR THIS MAGNIFICENT PRESENT, MOST VENERATED NEIGHBOR.

SO WUKONG GOT WHAT HE WANTED. DID HE GO HOME AFTERWARDS?

NOT RIGHT AWAY, FOR HE HAD OTHER DEMANDS.

HE ASKED THAT THE DRAGON KING GIVE HIM AN OUTFIT SUITED TO HIS NEW MAGIC STAFF.

THE KING CALLED UPON HIS BROTHERS AOQUIN, AOSHUN, AND AOJUN, RESPECTIVELY KINGS OF THE SOUTH, NORTH, AND WEST SEAS.

AND EACH ONE GAVE WUKONG THE ELEMENTS OF THE OUTFIT HE LONGED FOR.

HERE ARE MARVELOUS SANDALS OF LOTUS FIBER, MOST VENERATED "CONSCIOUS OF EMPTINESS."

I BRING YOU THIS INCOMPARABLE COAT OF MAIL OF SOLID GOLD.

AS FOR ME, I GIVE YOU THIS SPLENDID RED HELMET WITH PHOENIX WINGS.

I IMAGINE YOU'RE EXPECTING A DISPLAY OF GRATITUDE...

FOR NO ONE HAS EVER SEEN A MAMMAL-- THE MOST EVOLVED SPECIES IN NATURE-- THANK LIZARDS, WHICH ARE THE MOST BASIC.

AND YOU'LL WAIT A LONG TIME.

DISGRACEFUL!

CURSED MONKEY!

NEVER PLACE TRUST IN A CREATURE FROM THE SURFACE.

I SHALL AT ONCE COMPOSE A PETITION THAT I SHALL ADDRESS IN PERSON TO THE JADE EMPEROR...

THIS STAFF
BELONGS TO ME,
AND I AM ITS
SOLE MASTER!

THE DRAGON KING
THOUGHT HE WAS DUPING
ME BY OFFERING ME A
VULGAR HUNK OF
SCRAP-IRON.

BUT THIS STAFF
IS MAGICAL AND OBEYS
MY SLIGHTEST WORD.

O OUR
VENERATED KING,
SHOW US.

OH, YES, SHOW
US! SHOW US!

SHRINK,
SHRINK!

OOOOO!

GROW NOW!
GROW!

BIGGER!
EVEN BIGGER!

WHAT A DEVIL OF A MONKEY!

QUICKLY, TELL ME OF THE REST OF HIS ADVENTURES!

I CAN TELL YOU NOW THAT HE SHORTLY MET FRIENDS AS ASTONISHING AS HIS EXTRAORDINARY ENEMIES!

MY PARTNER'S EYES, HOWEVER, ARE CLOSING AND MY EARS ARE RINGING. FATIGUE IS ENVELOPING US.

AFTER OUR REST, COUNT ON US TO CAPTIVATE YOU WITH THE CONTINUATION OF THE INCREDIBLE ADVENTURES OF SU WUKONG, THE MONKEY KING!

END PART ONE

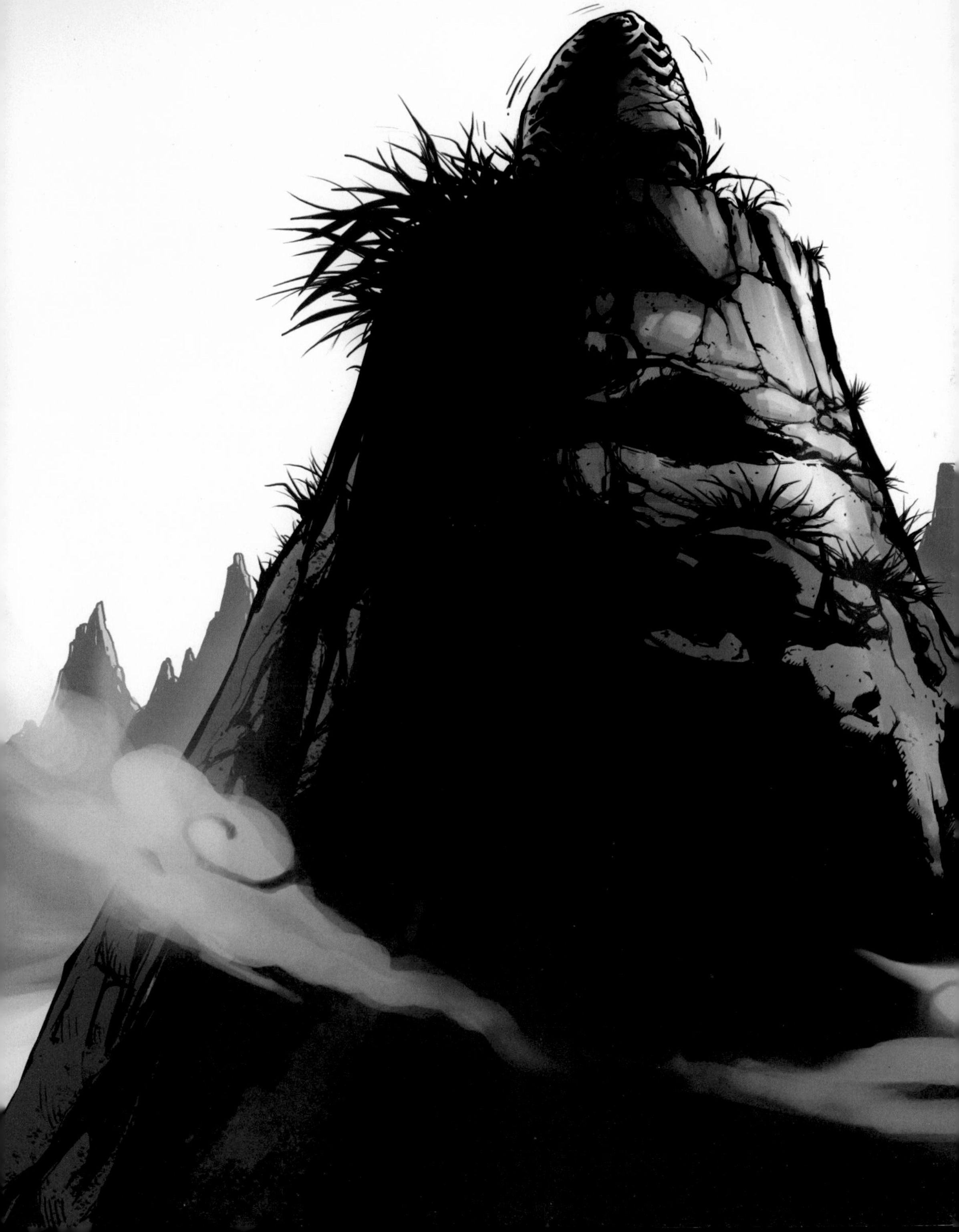

PART TWO

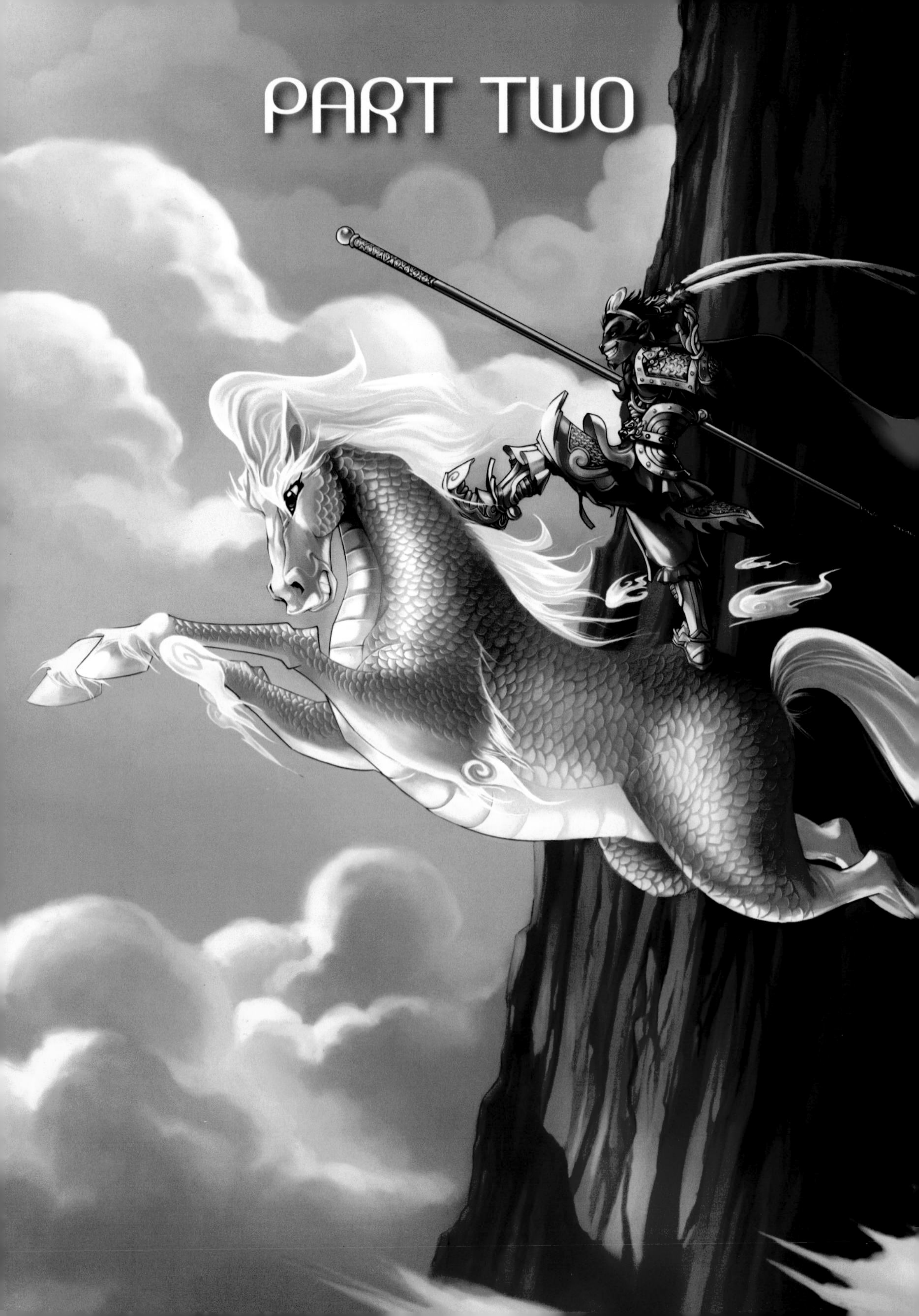

500 YEARS LATER...

SUN WUKONG!

YOUR MAJESTY, SOMEONE HAS COME UP TO OUR PALACE OF THE SOLAR STAR TO SEE YOU!

CURSED MONKEY!

CALM YOURSELF, YOUR MAJESTY, IT'S NOT IT'S HIM!

IT'S THE BODHISATTVA GUANYIN, SEEKING AN AUDIENCE.

SHE'S AWAITING YOU IN THE AUDIENCE ROOM.

LET'S GO...

MY RESPECTS, JADE EMPEROR.

I WARN YOU, HE'S BEEN SLEEPING POORLY FOR 500 YEARS. BE CAREFUL NOT TO ANGER HIM.

SPEAK CLEARLY, GUANYIN.

MAJESTY, I'VE COME TO SEEK YOUR PERMISSION TO LIBERATE SUN WUKONG...

...WHO HAS BEEN HELD PRISONER UNDER THE MOUNTAIN OF FIVE ELEMENTS.

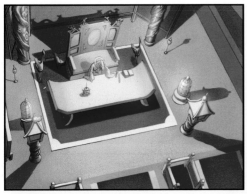

SUN... WU... KONG...

I'VE NOT FORGOTTEN THE BOTHER HE MANAGED TO CAUSE US.

COME NOW, YOU YOURSELF CAN'T BELIEVE YOUR WORDS.

DON'T YOU REMEMBER HOW THAT CURSED MONKEY ROILED THE HEAVENS?!

THE BOTHER? THAT'S PUTTING IT LIGHTLY, DEAR FRIEND!

THAT CURSED MONKEY ATTEMPTED TO SEIZE MY POSITION, AND WAS THE CAUSE OF THE GREATEST CELESTIAL WAR WE'VE EVER KNOWN!

YES, I REMEMBER THE DAY WHEN ALL OUR PROBLEMS BEGAN.

AOGUANG THE DRAGON KING AND QINGUANG THE JUDGE OF THE UNDERWORLD HAD COME TO BRING THEIR GRIEVANCES TO HIS MAJESTY.

QINGUANG LAMENTED THE DAY WHEN SUN WUKONG DESCENDED INTO THE UNDERWORLD TO ERASE HIS OWN NAME FROM THE BOOK OF THE DEAD!

AOGUANG PROTESTED AGAINST THE SACKING OF HIS PALACE BY THAT CURSED MONKEY!

I DECIDED TO SUMMON HIM TO THE HEAVENLY KINGDOM AND CONFERRED AN HONORABLE POSITION UPON HIM IN AN ATTEMPT TO BETTER CONTROL HIM.

WHAT A TERRIBLE IDEA!

I'D ENTRUSTED WUKONG WITH THE OFFICE OF THE PROTECTOR OF THE IMPERIAL HORSES. HE CONSIDERED THIS POSITION, HOWEVER, BENEATH HIM AND IMMEDIATELY ABANDONED IT!

WHAT A SCANDAL!

HE RETURNED TO HIS KINGDOM, WHERE HE PROCLAIMED HIMSELF "GREAT SAGE, EQUAL OF HEAVEN."

WHAT AUDACITY!

THEN, I DECIDED TO SEND CELESTIAL TROOPS COMMANDED BY THE KING LI DOOR PAGODA AND HIS SON, PRINCE NATA, TO THE MORTAL REALM IN ORDER TO CAPTURE THAT INSOLENT MONKEY.

WHAT A SPECTACLE!

THE MONKEY, NOT AT ALL ABASHED, REFUSED TO SURRENDER. HE DARED TO DEFY MY TROOPS!

WHAT A BATTLE!

EACH ONE STROVE INGENIOUSLY TO DOMINATE HIS FOE.

WHAT COMBAT!

A FORMIDABLE DUEL, INDEED, BUT ALAS, LOST BY NATA.

WHAT SHAME!

IN ANY CASE, I HAD TO FIND A SOLUTION TO SUBDUE THE REBEL!

SO I INVITED HIM AGAIN WITH GREAT POMP TO THE PALACE...

...CONFIRMED HIS TITLE OF "GREAT SAGE, EQUAL OF HEAVEN..."

...AND ENTRUSTED HIM WITH THE OFFICE OF GUARDIAN OF THE GROVE OF THE PEACHES OF IMMORTALITY.

WHAT AN HONOR!

WHAT AN ERROR!

AS SMART AS ENTRUSTING A JAR OF HONEY TO A BEAR!

That cursed monkey devoured all my fruit, which take thousands of years to ripen!

What a disaster!

Yes, and that's nothing compared to what followed...

The monster took offense for not having been invited to a party hosted by the Queen Mother of the Jade Pool.

What insolence!

Under the influence of drink, Wukong went to the Sovereign Lady's Palace...

...and made a mess of everything before the guests' arrival!

Then he dashed to the Palace of the Joyful, where he plucked the famous gourds filled with gold cinnabar...

...which confer immortality.

What a treasure!

BARBARIC APE! FLEEING THIEF!

HE MADE HIMSELF INVISIBLE TO ESCAPE HEAVEN AND RETURN TO HIS LAIR.

I DIDN'T KNOW THIS PART OF THE STORY. THAT DIABOLICAL MONKEY REALLY HAS MANY TRICKS UP HIS SLEEVE!

I HAD HAD ENOUGH AND NEEDED TO BE DONE WITH IT! I SENT AGAINST HIM ALL THE FORCES PRESENT IN HEAVEN, WHICH NUMBERED MORE THAN 100,000 WARRIORS!

WHAT A MULTITUDE!

AND IN HIS ANTIQUE ARMOR...

...THE MACAQUE WAS MARVELOUS!

HIS ARROGANCE CUT A FINE FIGURE.

HIS AUDACITY WAS WITHOUT PRECEDENT.

THAT BATTLE WAS A FRESCO...

...OF A TITANIC SIZE!

WITH THE HELP OF HIS TROOPS...

WUKONG ROUTED US FROM HIS LAND!

THEN, SUN WUKONG CHARGED AGAINST FOUR WARRIOR DIVINITIES.

TO SEND THEM TO THEIR GRAVES!

KING LI ATTEMPTED TO STOP WUKONG...

...BUT WAS CONQUERED IN ONE MOVE!

PRINCE NATA TRIED, TOO.

AND HE ENDED UP BADLY WOUNDED!

THE VICTORY WAS WON...

...BY THE MONKEY!

AN UNFORGET-TABLE DEFEAT.

HEAVEN WAS IN CRISIS!

OBSERVING THAT THE WAR HAD COME TO A STANDSTILL, I SUGGESTED THAT YOUR MAJESTY HAVE HIS NEPHEW ERLANG INTERVENE...

THE COMBAT WAS JUST AS MEMORABLE!

ERLANG'S ARMY ROUTED THOSE CURSED MONKEYS!

WHAT A DEBACLE!

HOWEVER, THE TWO GIANTS' STRENGTH WAS EQUAL, AND THE BATTLE'S OUTCOME REMAINED UNCERTAIN.

IT WAS LORD LAOZI WHO PUT AN END TO IT.

WHAT PRESENCE!

THANKS TO HIS MAGIC RING AND HIS HOUND XIQUAN...

...HE LAID LOW THE INDOMITABLE MONSTER.

WHAT AN OUTCOME!

ALAS, A TEMPORARY OUTCOME!

CONDEMNED TO CAPITAL PUNISHMENT BY ME, THE MACAQUE RESISTED ALL PUNISHMENT. THE PEACHES AND ELIXIR HAD MADE HIM IMMORTAL!

THAT'S INCREDIBLE!

HOW RESISTANT!

WHAT MELODRAMA!

WHAT LOVELY FLAMES!

IT'S INTERMINABLE...

BY THE END OF 49 DAYS, HE REEMERGED UNSCATHED FROM THE KILN OF TRANSFORMATION...

...AND GAVE THE CELESTIAL GUARDS A WALLOPING.

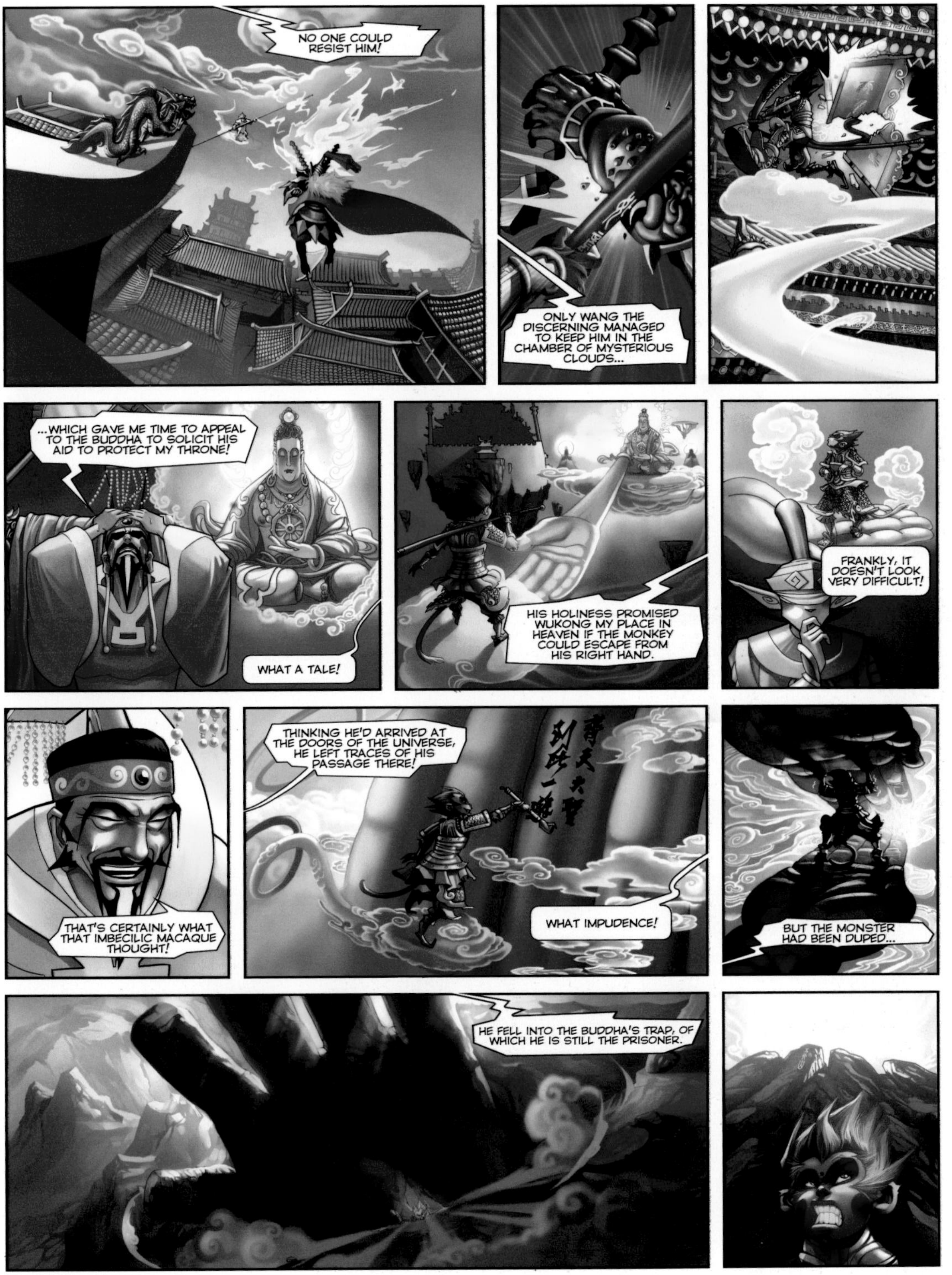
NO ONE COULD RESIST HIM!
ONLY WANG THE DISCERNING MANAGED TO KEEP HIM IN THE CHAMBER OF MYSTERIOUS CLOUDS...
...WHICH GAVE ME TIME TO APPEAL TO THE BUDDHA TO SOLICIT HIS AID TO PROTECT MY THRONE!
WHAT A TALE!
HIS HOLINESS PROMISED WUKONG MY PLACE IN HEAVEN IF THE MONKEY COULD ESCAPE FROM HIS RIGHT HAND.
FRANKLY, IT DOESN'T LOOK VERY DIFFICULT!
THAT'S CERTAINLY WHAT THAT IMBECILIC MACAQUE THOUGHT!
THINKING HE'D ARRIVED AT THE DOORS OF THE UNIVERSE, HE LEFT TRACES OF HIS PASSAGE THERE!
WHAT IMPUDENCE!
BUT THE MONSTER HAD BEEN DUPED...
HE FELL INTO THE BUDDHA'S TRAP, OF WHICH HE IS STILL THE PRISONER.

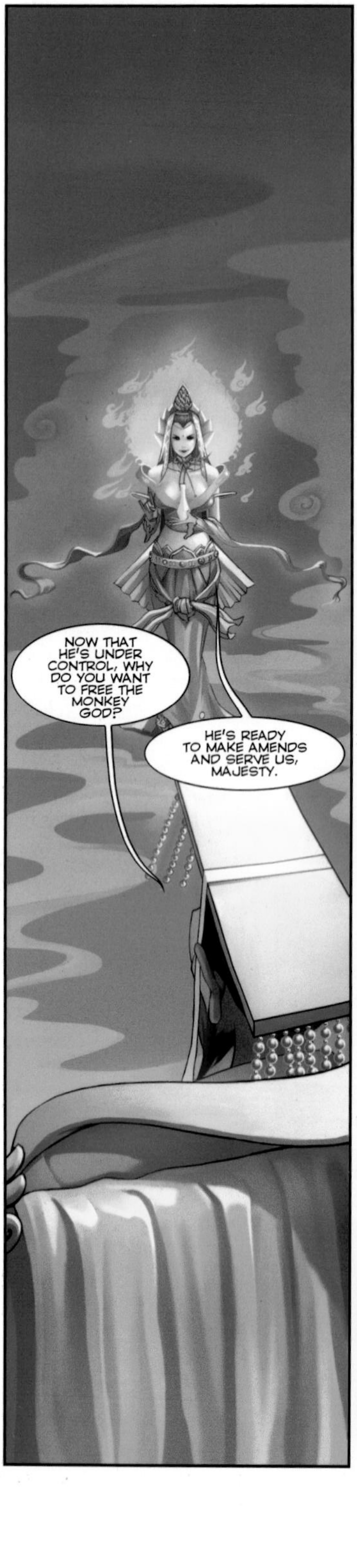
NOW THAT HE'S UNDER CONTROL, WHY DO YOU WANT TO FREE THE MONKEY GOD?
HE'S READY TO MAKE AMENDS AND SERVE US, MAJESTY.

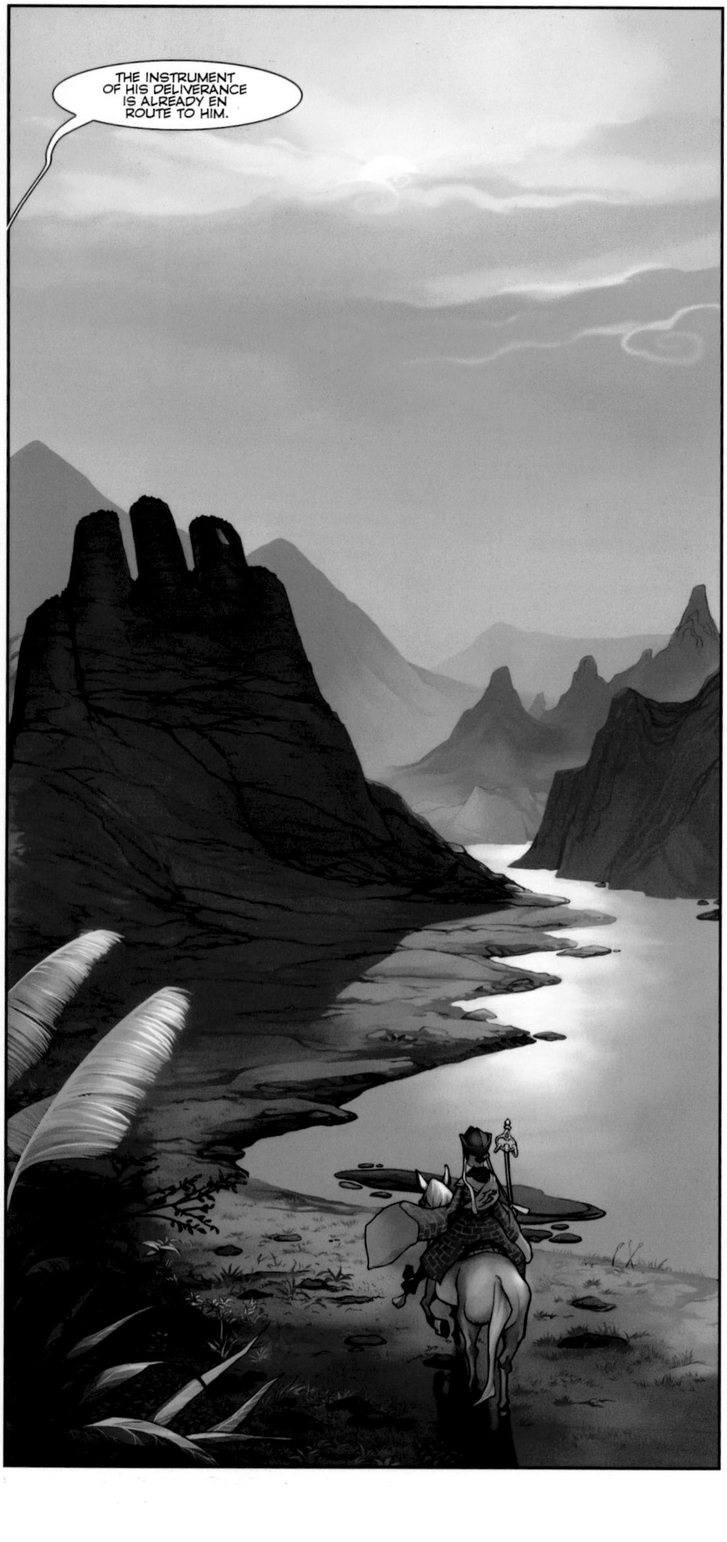
THE INSTRUMENT OF HIS DELIVERANCE IS ALREADY EN ROUTE TO HIM.

THIS WAY, MASTER! I'M HERE, IN THE ROCK!

ARE YOU XUANZANG, THE PILGRIM DEPARTING TO THE WEST ON A QUEST FOR SUTRAS?

HOW DO YOU KNOW THAT?

AH WELL, IT'S NONE TOO SOON! I'VE BEEN TRAPPED FOR 500 YEARS BY THESE INDESTRUCTIBLE ROCKS AND I'VE BEEN WAITING FOR YOU TO SET ME FREE. MY FOUR LIMBS ARE TINGLING!

SET YOU FREE? BUT HOW DO YOU WANT ME TO SHATTER THIS MOUNTAIN THAT YOU YOURSELF SAY IS INDESTRUCTIBLE?

...IT'S TRUE THAT THEY DON'T MISS ME... IT MUST BE SAID THAT I MADE A HUGE MESS IN HEAVEN. THEY PROBABLY REMEMBER THAT UP THERE!

AS THE JADE EMPEROR HAS NO SENSE OF HUMOR, HE ASKED THE BUDDHA TO CARVE THIS PRISON TO MY MEASURE.

THEN, SOME TIME AGO, I PROMISED THE BODHISATTVA GUANYIN TO BE WELL-BEHAVED IF SHE FREED ME. I SWORE TO SERVE YOU AND ACCOMPANY YOU INTO THE WEST IN THE QUEST FOR THE BUDDHA'S WRITINGS.

SHE TOLD ME THAT YOU SHOULD CLIMB TO THE TOP OF THE MOUNTAIN IN ORDER TO BREAK THE SEALS LAID THERE AND SET ME FREE.

INSCRIPTION ON THE TALISMAN: "O? MA?! PADME H??" (IN CHINESE. "IN EVERYTHING, EXISTS WAKEFULNESS.")

-HRRNN- IT FEELS GOOD TO STRETCH MY LEGS.

THANK YOU, MASTER. THANKS TO YOU, I'M FREE.

SO, WHAT'S YOUR NAME?

SUN WUKONG, MASTER.

ALSO KNOWN BY THE NAME OF GREAT SAGE, EQUAL OF HEAVEN!

THIS TIGER IS JUST IN TIME TO FURNISH ME WITH A NEW SUIT!

MASTER, WHILE I SKIN THIS TIGER, TELL ME OF THE PATH THAT BROUGHT YOU HERE?

IT ALL GOES BACK TO THE DAY WHEN EMPEROR TAIZHONG WAS REQUIRED TO APPEAR IN THE UNDERWORLD. HE'D PROMISED TO SPARE THE LIFE OF A DRAGON-KING, BUT PERJURED HIMSELF.

THANKS TO A RECOMMENDATION LETTER FROM HIS MINISTER, WEI-ZHENG, FOR THE JUDGE OF UNDERWORLD, THE EMPEROR OBTAINED A 20-YEAR REPRIEVE FROM DEATH.

GUIDED BY CUI-JUÉ ON THE PATH OF HIS RETURN TO LIFE, THE EMPEROR ESCAPED PROSECUTION BY TWO BROTHERS WHOM HE'D HAD ASSASSINATED.

THEN HE WAS RECEIVED BY THE 10 INFERNAL KINGS.

NEXT HE HAD TO TRAVERSE THE 18 HELLS...

...BEFORE CROSSING OVER THE BRIDGE OF NO RECOURSE, ESCORTED BY A GROUP OF PHANTOM SOLDIERS.

FINALLY, TAIZHONG ARRIVED IN THE CITY OF ILL DEATH, WHERE HE WAS ATTACKED BY A GROUP OF LOST SOULS AND PHANTOMS THAT WERE FATED TO WANDER.

THEY'D ONLY LET HIM RETURN TO LIFE WITH A SOLEMN PROMISE TO ORGANIZE A GRAND CEREMONY FOR THE SALVATION OF THE DECEASED.

AFTER HIS REBIRTH, THE EMPEROR DECIDED THAT, THIS TIME AROUND, HE'D HONOR ALL HIS COMMITMENTS AS SOON AS POSSIBLE.

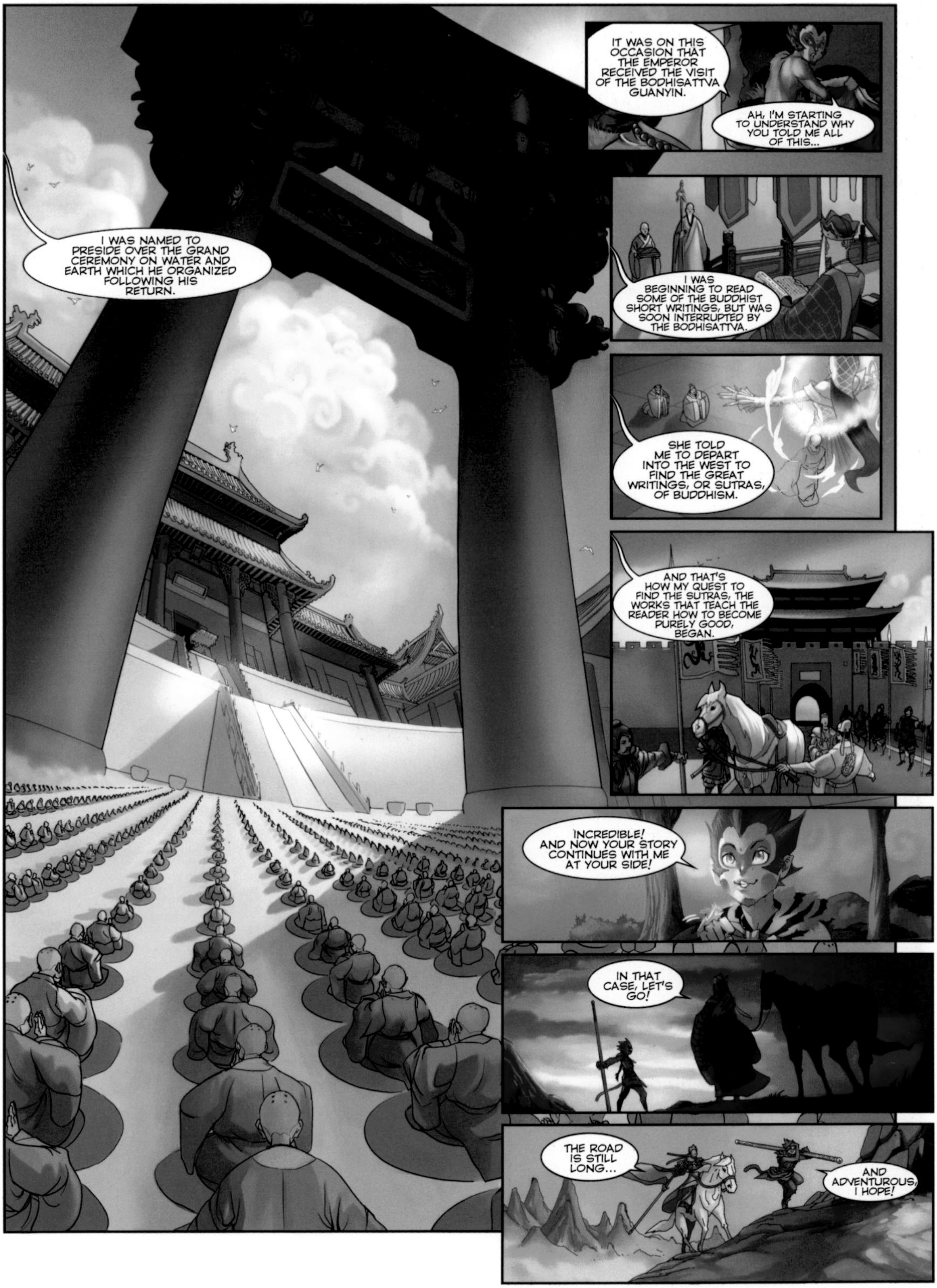

IT WAS ON THIS OCCASION THAT THE EMPEROR RECEIVED THE VISIT OF THE BODHISATTVA GUANYIN.
AH, I'M STARTING TO UNDERSTAND WHY YOU TOLD ME ALL OF THIS...
I WAS NAMED TO PRESIDE OVER THE GRAND CEREMONY ON WATER AND EARTH WHICH HE ORGANIZED FOLLOWING HIS RETURN.
I WAS BEGINNING TO READ SOME OF THE BUDDHIST SHORT WRITINGS, BUT WAS SOON INTERRUPTED BY THE BODHISATTVA.
SHE TOLD ME TO DEPART INTO THE WEST TO FIND THE GREAT WRITINGS, OR SUTRAS, OF BUDDHISM.
AND THAT'S HOW MY QUEST TO FIND THE SUTRAS, THE WORKS THAT TEACH THE READER HOW TO BECOME PURELY GOOD, BEGAN.
INCREDIBLE! AND NOW YOUR STORY CONTINUES WITH ME AT YOUR SIDE!
IN THAT CASE, LET'S GO!
THE ROAD IS STILL LONG...
AND ADVENTUROUS, I HOPE!

I'M GOING TO STARVE TO DEATH!

WE'RE ALL DOOMED!

THIS AREA IS TRULY DETESTABLE!

MORE THAN 2 WEEKS WITH NO TRAVELER TO LOOT...

AND NOTHING TO HUNT EITHER.

SHHH! SOMEONE'S COMING!

YOU SHOULD HAVE SEEN THE JADE EMPEROR'S FACE WHEN I GOBBLED UP HIS PEACHES...

IT WAS SO FUNNY!

EVEN THOUGH THE PUNISHMENT HE INFLICTED ON ME WAS EXCESSIVE, WELL, THAT'S JUST ANTI-MONKEY PREJUDICE!

HAVING ETERNITY BEFORE ONE, AND LEADING SUCH A MONOTONOUS LIFE...

WE'LL BREAK UP YOUR MONOTONY!

AND THE REST, TOO, IF YOU DON'T GIVE US EVERYTHING YOU HAVE ON YOU!

DON'T EVEN TRY TO FIGHT US!

WE'RE THE WORST BANDITS IN THE AREA!

OUR REPUTATION IS WELL-ESTABLISHED!

EVERYONE'S SCARED OF US!

FEAR NOT, MASTER. THESE GOOD FOLK HAVE SIMPLY COME TO BRING US SPARE GARMENTS AND FOOD.

YOU DON'T UNDERSTAND THAT THEY'RE THIEVES?

COME NOW, THEY LOOK MUCH TOO NICE FOR THAT.

THEY CAN HAVE NO OTHER INTENTION BESIDES WISHING TO SHARE THEIR POSSESSIONS WITH US.

TOO NICE?! US?

MY WORD, HE'S MOCKING US!

LET'S TEACH HIM SOME MANNERS!

WELL?

IT'S-- IT'S IMPOSSIBLE!

FLEE THE DEMON!!

I REALLY DON'T LIKE COWARDS...

SHALL WE LEAVE AGAIN, MASTER XUANZANG?

WHAT PROMPTED YOU TO TAKE THE LIVES OF THESE LOWLIFES, WHEN YOU COULD HAVE SIMPLY SCARED THEM AWAY?!

IF I HADN'T KILLED THEM, THEY MIGHT HAVE ATTACKED!

YOU'LL NEVER BE ABLE TO BECOME A MONK IF YOU CONTINUE TO PRACTICE ULTRA-VIOLENCE! HOW COULD I ACCEPT YOU ACCOMPANYING ME ON MY QUEST WITH SUCH A CRUEL TEMPERAMENT?

SINCE THAT'S HOW IT IS, I'M GIVING NOTICE!

I'M GOING HOME AND YOU CAN JUST CONTINUE BY YOURSELF!

MONKEYS AREN'T DOGS, AFTER ALL...

WHAT ARE YOU DOING ALONE IN THIS COUNTRY, VENERABLE SIR? ARE YOU LOST?

I'M ON A MISSION TO THE LANDS OF THE WEST, BUT I JUST LOST MY DISCIPLE.

HE GOT ANGRY FOLLOWING THE REMONSTRATIONS I ADDRESSED TO HIM AFTER HE KILLED THOSE WRETCHES FOR NO REASON.

AH, I KNOW AN UNSTOPPABLE MEANS TO BRING HIM TO HIS SENSES.

GET HIM TO SLIP ON THIS HAT OF SUBMISSION AND RECITE THIS INCANTATION. HE WILL OBEY YOU.

ALAS, I'M NEVER GOING TO SEE HIM AGAIN! I DON'T EVEN KNOW WHERE HE WENT.

BE WITHOUT FEAR, VENERABLE ONE. I'LL MAKE SURE HE COMES BACK TO YOU.

THE BODHISATTVA!

I'M SO UNWORTHY FOR NOT HAVING RECOGNIZED HER...

MY LITTLE ONES, HOW HAPPY THEY'LL BE TO SEE ME AGAIN.

THAT TIME WITHOUT ME MUST HAVE--

BODHISATTVA GUANYIN?

SUN WUKONG, WHAT ARE YOU DOING HERE WHEN YOU SHOULD BE WITH XUANZANG?

?PPPT! THAT MONK UNDERSTANDS NOTHING AT ALL, ALTHOUGH I WAS DOING MY UTMOST TO PROTECT HIM. HE REPROACHED ME FOR SLAYING HIS ASSAILANTS.

SUN WUKONG, DON'T COMPROMISE YOUR CHANCES OF SALVATION OVER A BIT OF ILL HUMOR, OTHERWISE YOU'LL NEVER FIND THE WAY.

IF YOU DON'T OBEY YOUR MASTER AND DON'T RETURN TO HIM, YOU WILL REMAIN A PERVERSE BEING...

...FOR ETERNITY.

ALL RIGHT, WORRY NO FURTHER ABOUT IT, YOU'VE WON! I'LL GO BACK.

HURRY UP!

WITHOUT YOU, HE'S FAR TOO VULNERABLE...

MASTER, YOUR GOOD OLD SUN WUKONG IS BACK!

AFTER ABANDONING ME IN A COWARDLY FASHION, WHY ARE YOU COMING BACK NOW?

I ONLY WANTED TO SAY HELLO TO MY DEAR, LITTLE MONKEYS, BUT I CHANGED MY MIND EN ROUTE!

WHAT'S MORE, THAT JAUNT HAS GIVEN ME AN APPETITE!

YOU HAVE ONLY TO DIG THROUGH THE BAG OF PROVISIONS. THERE MUST STILL BE A FEW CAKES THERE.

OH, WHAT A PRETTY HAT! I'VE NEVER SEEN ANYTHING LIKE IT BEFORE!

I GREW WEARY OF IT. TAKE IT, IF YOU LIKE.

NICE! I'M A HANDSOME DEVIL!

MASTER, WHAT'S HAPPENING? IT'S BURNING MY SKULL, IT'S HORRIBLE!

DO YOU SWEAR TO ME YOU'LL BEHAVE YOURSELF AND OBEY ME?

YES, YES, ANYTHING YOU LIKE, BUT STOP!

GOOD, I TRUST YOU. BUT KNOW THAT I CAN REACTIVATE IT AT ANY MOMENT!

∋HFPTTT...ε

ALL RIGHT, LET'S GO.

AND HURRY UP A BIT, OR--

COMING RIGHT AWAY, MASTER!

HOW THE DEVIL WILL WE CROSS OVER?

WE HAVE ONLY TO USE MY MAGIC CLOUD!

COME NOW, YOU KNOW FULL WELL THAT SUCH CONVENIENCES FURTHER REMOVE US FROM THE PATH TO ENLIGHTENMENT!

AH, YES, I'D FORGOTT--?!

A-- A DRAGON!

WHAT ILL LUCK! WITHOUT A HORSE, OUR QUEST IS OVER!

HE GOBBLED DOWN OUR MARE!

I'LL BREAK THAT ANIMAL IN.

HEY, YOU, HORRIBLE SERPENT! SHOW YOURSELF BEFORE I COME FISH YOU OUT SO YOU CAN FEEL THE WEIGHT OF MY STAFF!

WHERE ARE YOU GOING NOW, CURSED MACAQUE?

I'VE ALREADY CONQUERED DRAGONS-- BIGGER ONES THAN YOU!

THE GODDESS!

AH, YOU'RE JUST IN TIME! I HAVE SOMETHING TO SAY TO YOU!

I'M SURE IT'S YOU WHO ENTRUSTED HIM WITH THIS HAT THAT KEEPS ME AT HIS MERCY! DID I NOT GIVE YOU MY WORD TO HELP HIM ACCOMPLISH HIS QUEST?

WITHOUT THAT HAT, YOU'RE UNCONTROLLABLE, FOR YOU CANNOT DISTINGUISH THE GOOD FROM THE BAD-- AND MUCH LESS WHAT IS CHANCE AND WHAT IS OF THE QUEST!

THAT CREATURE-- LIKE YOU-- HAS FAULTS TO EXPIATE, WHICH IT WILL DO BY ACCOMPANYING YOU ON YOUR JOURNEY INTO THE WEST.

IF YOU WANT TO HELP THE MONK, WHY DID YOU LET THAT CURSED DRAGON EAT HIS HORSE?

?!

?!

AORUN, SHOW YOURSELF!

GUANYIN IS HERE AND WANTS TO SEE YOU.

WHAT A SUBLIME SPECTACLE!

BAH, I'VE DONE BETTER...

AORUN, HENCEFORTH YOU WILL ACCOMPANY XUANZANG AND HIS NOVICE ON THEIR QUEST.

NOW YOU ARE READY TO RESUME YOUR JOURNEY. THE ROUTE THAT LEADS YOU TO THE HOLY WRITINGS, HOWEVER, IS BESTREWN WITH TRIALS.

THESE HAIRS CAN TRANSFORM THEMSELVES AND SAVE YOU IN CASE OF GREAT DANGER.

OUCH! CAREFUL, THAT STINGS!

GODDESS, DO NOT LEAVE! I HAVEN'T EVEN HAD TIME TO THANK YOU...

...GOODBYE.

STILL, THAT HORSE CAN'T TELL US HOW TO GET ACROSS THIS RIVER.

WAIT, I'LL GO ASK THAT FISHERMAN FOR HELP.

I HADN'T IMAGINED SUCH A GRANDIOSE CROSSING...

ALL THE SAME, WHERE DID THAT FISHERMAN COME FROM? THERE WAS NARY A SOUL ON THE WATER A MOMENT BEFORE!

YOU KNOW, SOMETIMES, YOU MUST BE ABLE TO TRUST IN DESTINY WITHOUT ASKING QUESTIONS.

IT SEEMS LIKE THAT CURSED MONKEY HAS STARTED TO BE REASONABLE!

DON'T BE SO SURE, YOUR MAJESTY! SINCE THEN, HE HAS BEEN THE CAUSE OF MANY MORE WORRIES FOR THE MONK!

FOR A WHILE, THEY'D STOPPED AT A MONASTERY TO REQUEST ROOM AND BOARD...

...THAT VAIN MONKEY COULDN'T KEEP HIMSELF FROM VAUNTING THE BEAUTY OF THE KASAYA ROBE ENTRUSTED TO XUANZANG BY GUANYIN.

UPON SIGHT OF IT, THE PATRIARCH COULDN'T RESIST THE DESIRE TO POSSESS IT.

WHEN NIGHT CAME, THE GREEDY OLD MAN, ELIMINATED THE TRAVELERS.

SUN WUKONG SENSED THE TRAP COMING, HOWEVER, AND WAS ALREADY PREPARED.

BEFORE FALLING ASLEEP, HE'D CLIMBED UP TO HEAVEN TO BORROW A FIRE-RESISTANT LID.

HE TURNED THE FIRE AGAINST THE MONASTERY AND SAVED HIS MASTER.

BUT WHOLLY OCCUPIED AS HE WAS BY THIS TASK, HE DIDN'T NOTICE THE ARRIVAL OF THE BLACK WIND MONSTER, WHICH WAS ALERTED BY THE GLARE.

THE MONSTER PROFITED FROM CONFUSION TO TAKE THE ROBE.

EATEN UP WITH SHAME, THE PATRIARCH DIED BY HIS OWN HAND. THE ROBE, HOWEVER, WAS NOWHERE TO BE FOUND.

THEN, THE MONKEY FOUND THE TRACES LEFT BY BLACK WIND AND REALIZED THAT THE MONSTER HAD PURLOINED THE OBJECT.

WITHOUT WAITING, HE LEARNED OF THE LOCATION OF THE LAIR AND DEPARTED TOWARDS THE BLACK WIND MOUNTAIN.

THEY WERE EVENLY MATCHED.

THE COMBAT WAS TITANIC...

HE REQUESTED THE HELP OF THE BODHISATTVA GUANYIN...

AFTER A FEW DAYS, SUN WUKONG DECIDED TO CHANGE TACTICS.

...AND SHE GRANTED HIS REQUEST.

SHE SUBDUED THE MONSTER WITH A CONSTRICTING CIRCLE!

HE WASTES NO OCCASION TO CALL UPON YOU.

SUN WUKONG THEN RETURNED TO HIS MASTER'S SIDE, AND THEY RESUMED THEIR ROUTE TOWARDS THE WEST.

MASTER, ALL THESE NIGHTS SPENT SLEEPING OUTSIDE HAVE MADE ME YEARN FOR THE COMFORT OF A GOOD BED.

WHAT IF WE SOUGHT THE HOSPITALITY OF THAT FARM?

GOOD IDEA! CONSIDERING THE HOUR, I WOULD APPRECIATE A MEAL.

THERE'S NOBODY AROUND TO WELCOME US.

HELLO, ANYBODY?! WE'RE PILGRIMS GOING TO THE WEST, IN SEARCH OF HOLY WRITINGS!

CRY OUT IF YOU MUST, BUT DO IT SILENTLY SO YOU DO NOT DISTURB ANYONE.

IS THIS HOW THIS TOWN WELCOMES VISITORS?!

YOU'VE COME AT A BAD TIME, WORTHY VOYAGERS. MASTER GAO CANNOT RECEIVE YOU.

HE IS UNDER THE HEEL OF A MONSTER THAT'S TERRORIZING THE HOUSE. AND HE DOESN'T KNOW HOW TO BE RID OF IT.

ON THE CONTRARY, YOU COULDN'T HAVE HOPED FOR A BETTER GUEST.

I'M USED TO HUNTING MONSTERS...

PLEASE EXCUSE THIS MODEST WELCOME. I KNOW IT IS UNWORTHY OF YOUR RANK, BUT IT IS A DIFFICULT TIME FOR OUR HOUSEHOLD.

THIS UGLY LITTLE THING SAYS IT IS ABLE TO RID US OF THE MONSTER THAT'S TERRORIZING US?

DON'T MISJUDGE HIS APPEARANCE. THIS MONKEY CAN DO GREAT THINGS WHEN HE IS INCLINED TO!

NOW, TELL US OF YOUR MISFORTUNES.

THREE YEARS AGO, A FELLOW CAME TO SETTLE DOWN HERE. I MARRIED HIM TO MY DAUGHTER, BLUE ORCHID...

AT FIRST, MY SON-IN-LAW, ROBUS, DID THE WORK OF TEN MEN BY HIMSELF!

BUT ONE DAY HE STARTED CHANGING INTO A PIG!

HE ALSO BECAME A PIG. AN INSATIABLE GLUTTON, HE SEIZED ALL MY WEALTH, AND NONE OF US DARES TO DEFY HIM, FOR HE POSSESSES TERRIFYING POWERS!

MY REPUTATION IS RUINED IN ALL THE REGION. THAT MEANS NOTHING COMPARED TO THE FACT--

--THAT HE'S BEEN HOLDING MY DAUGHTER PRISONER FOR SIX MONTHS.

I DON'T EVEN KNOW IF SHE'S STILL ALIVE.

HE'S IN THERE.

THE MONSTER DISAPPEARS DURING THE DAY AND ONLY RETURNS AT NIGHT.

HMM, THE DOOR LOOKS SOLID...

...UNLIKE THE WALL SUPPORTING IT!

BLUE ORCHID?

IT'S ME, YOUR FATHER.

PAPA? IS IT REALLY YOU?

PAP--?

FATHER?

YOU'RE ALIVE! I DIDN'T EXPECT TO SEE YOU AGAIN.

GO CONCEAL YOURSELF WHILE I WAIT FOR YOUR PIG MONSTER... AND REASSEMBLE THE WALLS BEFORE LEAVING!

WE NEED TO MAKE SURE HE DOESN'T REALIZE ANYTHING IS WRONG WHEN HE RETURNS TONIGHT.

LET'S HURRY. EVERYTHING MUST BE READY BEFORE NIGHTFALL!

THE ELEMENT OF SURPRISE IS VITAL.

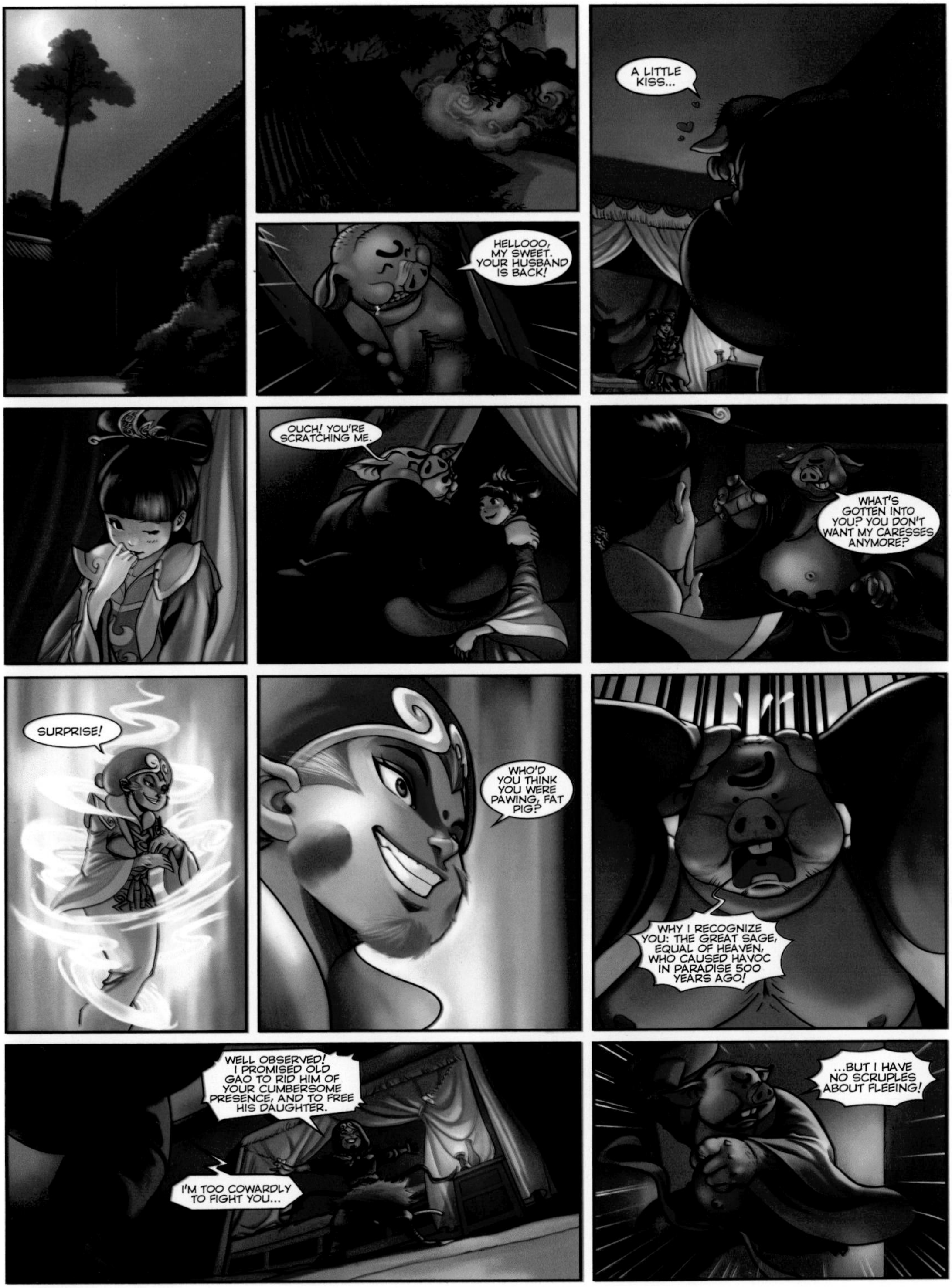
HELLOOO, MY SWEET. YOUR HUSBAND IS BACK!
A LITTLE KISS...
OUCH! YOU'RE SCRATCHING ME.
WHAT'S GOTTEN INTO YOU? YOU DON'T WANT MY CARESSES ANYMORE?
SURPRISE!
WHO'D YOU THINK YOU WERE PAWING, FAT PIG?
WHY I RECOGNIZE YOU: THE GREAT SAGE, EQUAL OF HEAVEN, WHO CAUSED HAVOC IN PARADISE 500 YEARS AGO!
WELL OBSERVED! I PROMISED OLD GAO TO RID HIM OF YOUR CUMBERSOME PRESENCE, AND TO FREE HIS DAUGHTER.
I'M TOO COWARDLY TO FIGHT YOU...
...BUT I HAVE NO SCRUPLES ABOUT FLEEING!

I'LL PURSUE YOU TO THE UNDERWORLD IF I HAVE TO!

YOU WON'T ESCAPE ME!

I DON'T BELIEVE IT!

HEY, LARD-BUTT, DO YOU THINK YOU CAN ESCAPE ME BY HIDING?

THIS CAVE IS A DEAD-END. I'LL DRIVE YOU OUT.

TOO BAD FOR YOU!

NOTHING IS MORE TERRIFYING THAN A CORNER-ED PIG!

-BRRR- I'M AFRAID!

DID YOU KNOW THAT, BEFORE BECOMING WHAT I AM, I HAD A PLACE AMONG THE GODS?

YOU MAKE ME LAUGH! I KNOW ALL OF THEM, AND I DON'T REMEMBER EVER HAVING MET YOU.

I HELD A HIGH OFFICE AND COMMANDED THE NAVAL FORCES OF THE MILKY WAY!

I REMEMBER WHEN THEY ATTACKED THE MOUNTAIN OF FLOWERS AND FRUITS, MY LITTLE MONKEYS MADE A PASTE OUT OF THEM!

-OINK!- CURSED MACAQUE, I'LL MAKE YOU SWALLOW YOUR INSULTS!

HA HA HA!
THAT'S THE COST
OF CONFRONTING
THE GREAT SAGE,
EQUAL OF
HEAVEN!

YOU
SHOULD
KEEP YOUR
RAKE FOR
GARDENING!

~-OINK~-, WHAT INSOLENCE! I DON'T UNDERSTAND WHY THE JADE EMPEROR GAVE YOU BACK YOUR FREEDOM!

IT WAS THE BODHISATTVA GUANYIN WHO OBTAINED IT.

IN EXCHANGE, I'M ACCOMPANYING THE MONK XUANZANG INTO THE WEST ON A QUEST TO FIND THE HOLY WRITINGS OF THE BUDDHA.

THE MONK IS WITH YOU?

LET'S STOP FIGHTING. I SURRENDER.

WHAT IS THIS RUSE? ARE YOU LOOKING FOR A NEW WAY TO ESCAPE?

THE GODDESS ALSO MADE ME PROMISE TO ACCOMPANY THE PILGRIM ON THE QUEST FOR SUTRAS. IT'S THE ONLY WAY I HAVE TO ATONE FOR THE FAULTS THAT EARNED ME THE DISHONOR IN WHICH I FIND MYSELF!

I SWEAR BEFORE HEAVEN THAT I'M TELLING THE TRUTH!

THEN YOU WON'T HESITATE TO BURN YOUR HOUSE TO PROVE YOUR SINCERITY? IF YOU DO, I'LL LEAD YOU TO MY MASTER.

MASTER, HERE I AM! I BRING YOU THE MONSTER, SUBDUED.

MASTER, I SWORE TO THE BODHISATTVA GUANYIN TO SERVE YOU AND TO ACCOMPANY YOU ON YOUR QUEST.

WHY WERE YOU PUNISHED?

WHEN I WAS STILL THE LEADER OF THE NAVAL FORCES OF THE MILKY WAY, I DISRESPECTED A PRETTY FAIRY DURING THE FEAST OF THE IMMORTAL PEACHES.

AS PUNISHMENT, I WAS BANISHED FROM HEAVEN AND TRANSFORMED INTO A PIG. I HAD TO PROMISE TO AWAIT YOUR COMING.

I BEG YOU TO PLEASE ACCEPT ME AS A DISCIPLE!

THAT'S PERFECT! HENCEFORTH, I GIVE YOU THE NAME OF ZHU BAJIE "EIGHT DEFENSES," AND YOU'LL BECOME MY SECOND DISCIPLE!

I'M DELIGHTED TO SEE HIM DEVOTE HIMSELF TO GOODNESS AGAIN! I'M CERTAIN THAT ZHU BAJIE WILL BE OF PRECIOUS HELP TO YOU ON YOUR TREK.

BLUE ORCHID...

MOUNT STOUPA!

HERE'S WHERE THE MASTER OF THE CROWS' NEST LIVES.

DO YOU KNOW HIM?

YES. HE ASKED ME TO BECOME HIS DISCIPLE IN ORDER TO STUDY THE WAY BUT I LACKED THE COURAGE.

WELL, WELL...

BE WELCOME, PILGRIMS. I WAS EXPECTING YOU.

HELLO, ZHU BAJIE. I'M DELIGHTED TO SEE YOU'VE CONVERTED TO THE GOOD.

THE MASTER HAS A GIFT FOR KNOWING THE FUTURE.

MASTER, COULD YOU TELL US IF THE ROAD WEST IS A LONG ONE YET?

VERY LONG, YES! MANY DANGERS AWAIT YOU.

THE WORST PERILS ARE RESERVED FOR YOU BY THE DEMON OF ILLUSION. THE HEART SUTRA CAN PROTECT YOU.

I IMPLORE YOU TO TEACH IT TO ME, MASTER.

THANKS BE TO YOU. I PROMISE YOU TO MAKE GOOD USE OF IT.

AND WHAT ROAD MUST WE FOLLOW TO THE WEST?

FOR THE ROAD, LET YOURSELF BE LED, THE STONE MONKEY KNOWS THE WAY! BUT CAREFUL: MOUNTAINS, RIVERS, TIGERS, FOXES, AND LEOPARDS WILL BE YOUR ENEMIES.

THE STONE MONKEY, BUT THAT'S ME?! I DON'T KNOW THE WAY... WHAT COULD HE HAVE MEANT?

ALL RIGHT, LET'S GO!

WHAT'S THE NEWS OF SUN WUKONG AND HIS COMPANIONS?

THEY'VE JUST LEFT THE YELLOW WIND MOUNTAIN, MAJESTY.

THERE'S A MONSTER IN THAT REGION WHO SHARES A NAME WITH THE MOUNTAIN, ISN'T THERE?

THERE WAS! OUR PILGRIMS CHASED IT AWAY.

YELLOW WIND WAS THE LORD OF THAT DANGEROUS COUNTRY.

UPON ARRIVING, OUR MONKS ENCOUNTERED HIS FAITHFUL LIEUTENANT, WHO GAVE THE TRAVELERS A VIOLENT WELCOME!

SEEING THAT HE WAS NO MATCH FOR SUN WUKONG AND ZHU BAIJE, HE ESCAPED THEM BY A SKILLFUL RUSE, LEAVING HIS SKIN UPON A ROCK.

THE LIEUTENANT TOOK ADVANTAGE OF THE DISCIPLES' CONFUSION. HE ABDUCTED XUANZANG AND TOOK HIM TO HIS MASTER.

THE BATTLE BEGAN.

SUN WUKONG FOUGHT VALIANTLY...

...AND ZHU BAJIE QUICKLY RAKED UP HIS ENEMIES.

THE SURVIVORS FLED TO WARN THEIR MASTER OF THE DISASTER THAT WAS APPROACHING.

THEN YELLOW WIND IN PERSON THREW HIMSELF INTO THE BATTLE!

YELLOW WIND WON THAT ROUND.

A GOOD NIGHT'S REST ALLOWED OUR MONKEY TO BE TREATED BY THE KINDLY LOCAL DIVINITIES.

AND THE NEXT DAY, TRANSFORMED INTO A MOSQUITO, HE RETURNED TO THE MONSTER'S LAIR, QUITE DETERMINED TO FIND ITS WEAK POINT.

AFTER GATHERING THE INFORMATION, SUN WUKONG LEFT TO ASK FOR THE HELP OF A LOCAL SAINT, WHO POSSESSED THE SPIRIT OF A DRAGON.

THE FIGHT WAS SWIFT.

AFTER FREEING THEIR MASTER, OUR PILGRIMS RESUMED THEIR JOURNEY INTO THE WEST.

ALL'S WELL THAT ENDS WELL.

WHERE ARE THEY NOW?

IN THE VICINITY OF THE RIVER OF MOVING SANDS.

DEADLY WATERS OF AN INFINITE DEPTH, WHICH NO ONE CAN CROSS.

I DON'T LIKE PONDS...

WE ESCAPED JUST TO END UP HERE! WHAT MISFORTUNE!

AT LEAST THE RIVER DRAGON WAS CALM--?!

WHAT THE--?

LOOK OUT!

WHO ARE YOU WHO DARES COME TO ATTACK US?

KNOW THAT YOU'RE SPEAKING TO AN IMPORTANT DIGNITARY WHO ONCE HAD A PLACE AT THE COURT OF THE JADE EMPEROR!

YOU MUSTN'T BE SO IRREPLACE-ABLE TO FIND YOURSELF EXILED HERE!

YOU'LL PAY FOR THAT AFFRONT.

WAIT FOR US HERE. I'M GOING TO RELIEVE THAT INCOMPETENT ZHU BAJIE!

YOU FOOL, WHY DID YOU POKE YOUR NOSE IN?

A FEW MORE PASSES AND HE WOULD HAVE BEEN DONE FOR!

COME NOW, PIGLET, DON'T BE MAD! YOU'LL SOON HAVE THE OCCASION TO BRING DOWN OTHER VILLAINS WHO ARE MUCH FATTER AND STRONGER THAN HIM.

WELL, MY DISCIPLES, HAVE YOU GOTTEN RID OF THE CREATURE?

WE GAVE IT SUCH A SCARE THAT IT RAN AWAY, MASTER!

TOO BAD! IF YOU TWO HAD CAPTURED IT, WE COULD HAVE USED IT TO CROSS THIS RIVER OF A THOUSAND DANGERS.

THE MASTER IS RIGHT, PIGLET. GO INTO THE DEPTHS TO DRIVE IT OUT.

ONCE YOU'VE PUSHED IT BACK TO THE SURFACE, I'LL TAKE CARE OF CAPTURING IT

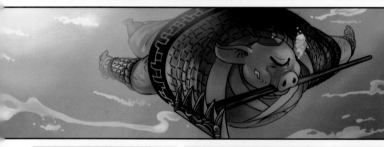

?!

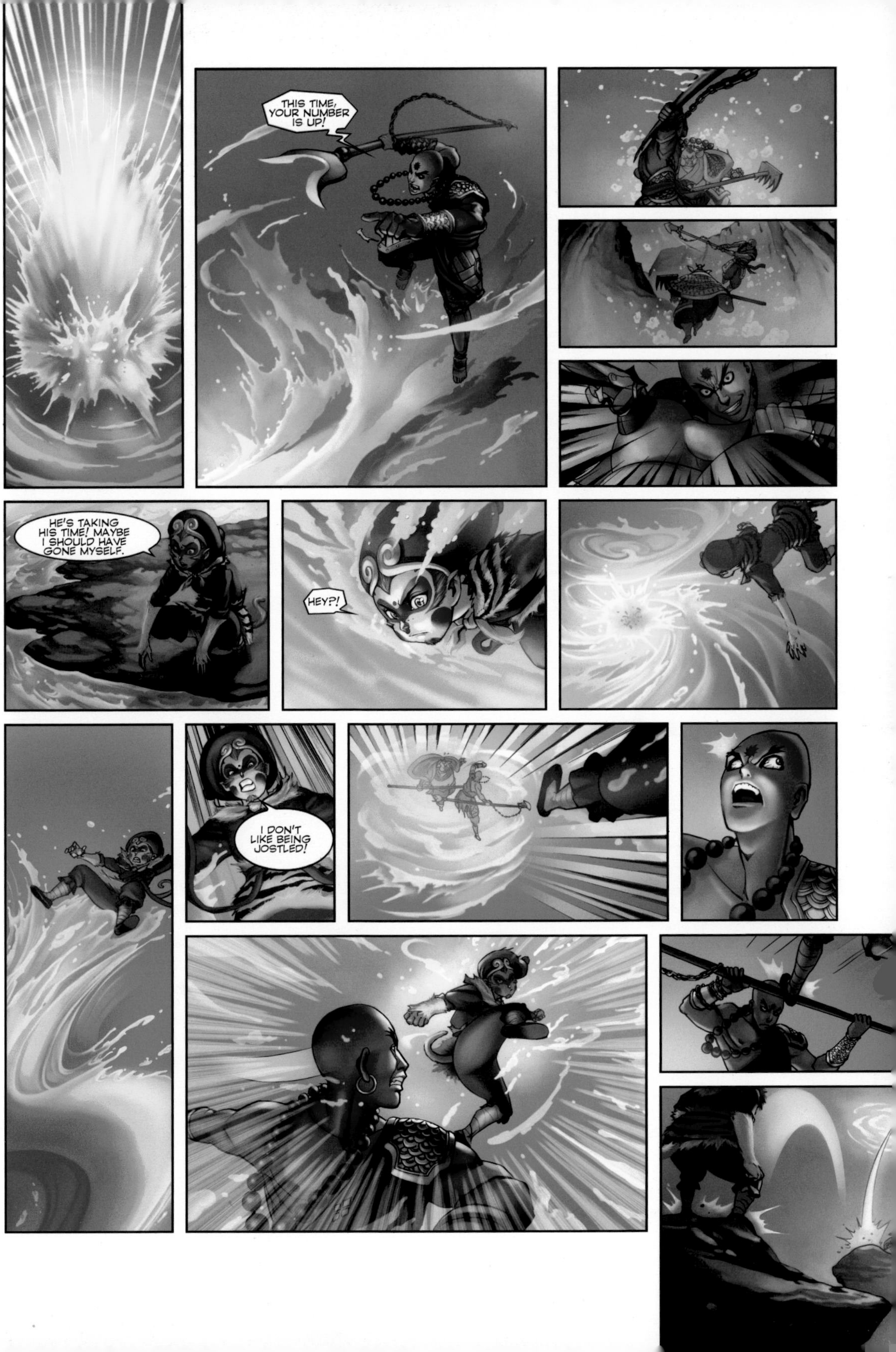
THIS TIME, YOUR NUMBER IS UP!
HE'S TAKING HIS TIME! MAYBE I SHOULD HAVE GONE MYSELF.
HEY?!
I DON'T LIKE BEING JOSTLED!

TRULY, YOU'RE DOING IT ON PURPOSE.

I ADMIT THAT THIS SHASENG IS PERPLEXING...

NOW THAT I THINK ABOUT IT, THANKS TO OUR MAGICAL CLOUDS, WE COULD EASILY BRING OUR MASTER ACROSS THIS CURSED RIVER!

YOU COULD EVEN GO DIRECTLY TO THE PARADISE IN THE WEST, ASK THE BUDDHA FOR THE SUTRAS, AND BRING THEM BACK TO US.

POOR FOOL, YOU KNOW NOTHING! I'M FORBIDDEN TO DO ALL THAT.

SUN WUKONG EXPLAINED TO ZHU BAJIE THAT XUANZANG MUST PERSONALLY UNDERGO ALL THE TRIALS THAT LEAD TO THE LANDS OF THE WEST. THAT IT WAS ON THIS CONDITION ALONE THAT THE HOLY WRITINGS WOULD BE GIVEN TO HIM.

TRULY, THAT MONKEY STILL SURPRISES ME. HE'S SHOWING MORE CLEAR-SIGHTEDNESS THAN I'D HAVE BELIEVED.

WHAT'S THE SITUATION WITH OUR PILGRIMS NOW?

THEY'RE AWAITING THE RETURN OF SUN WUKONG, WHO'S GONE TO ASK GUANYIN'S HELP TO VANQUISH THE MONSTER, SHASENG.

I'M REALLY WONDERING HOW THIS WILL ALL TURN OUT!

END PART TWO

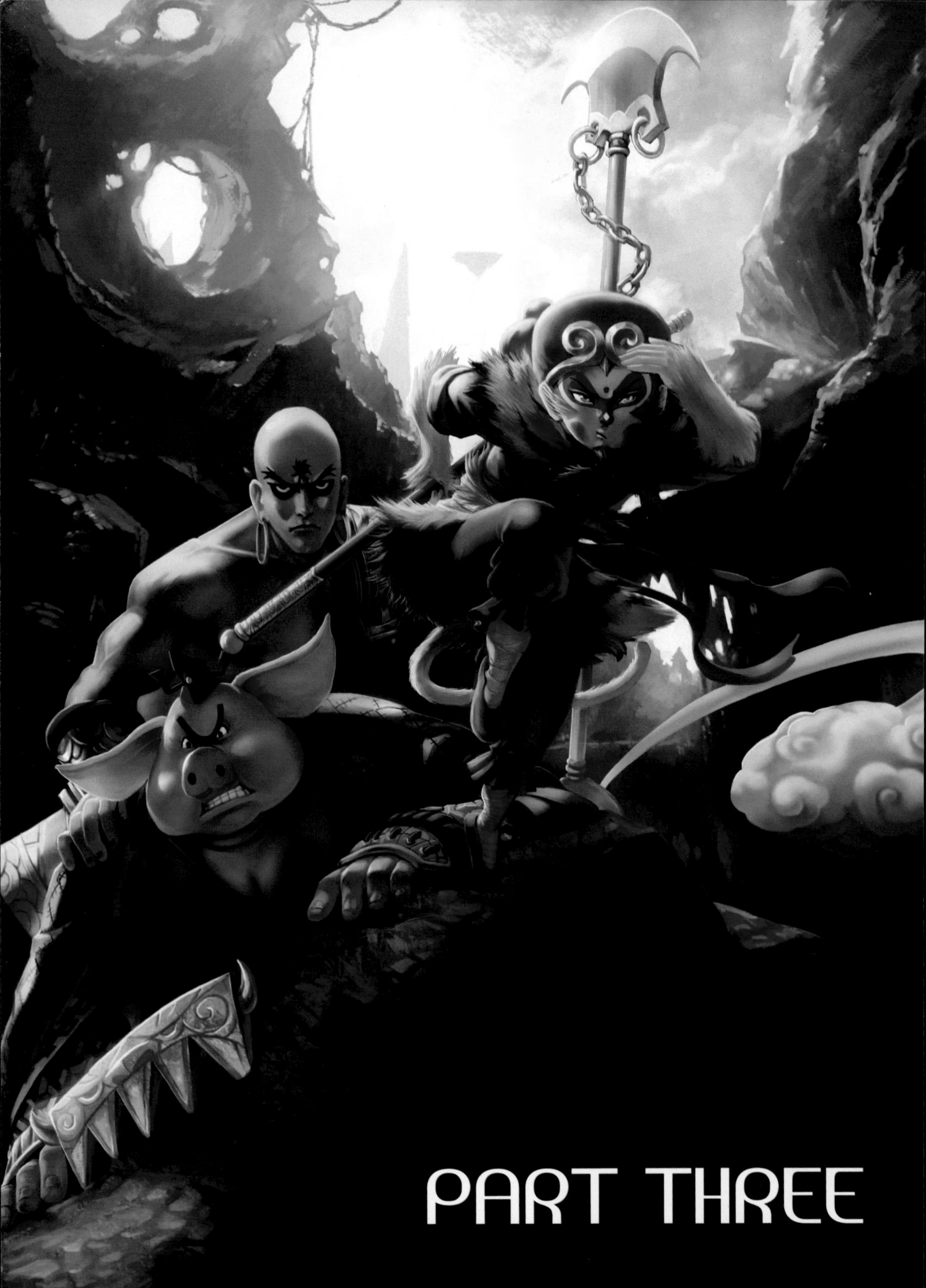

PART THREE

AY YI YI! ALREADY ELEVEN O'CLOCK! I'M LATE! I SLEPT LIKE A LOG...

I DIDN'T HEAR THE MORNING GONG!

I MUST HAVE OVERDONE IT LAST NIGHT ON THE PEACHES OF IMMORTALITY JUICE.

AND THOUSAND-LEAGUE EYE, DIDN'T BOTHER STOPPING ME!

THE TART! BY NOW, SHE MUST ALREADY BE SIMPERING AROUND THE EMPEROR. >GRRR!<

OHHHH!

THAT DAMNED MACAQUE!

OHHHH!

...ON HIS MAGIC CLOUD EN ROUTE TO MOUNT POTALAKA TO REQUEST HELP FROM THE BODHISATTVA GUANYIN.

WHY DID SUN WUKONG GO TO SEEK THE GODDESS' HELP?

REMEMBER, OUR PILGRIMS HAD ARRIVED AT THE OUTSKIRTS OF THE LAKE OF MOVING SANDS.

BUT SHASENG, THE RIVER MONSTER, ATTACKED THEM.

UNDERSTANDING HE COULD NOT VANQUISH SUCH POWERFUL ADVERSARIES, SHASENG HID AMID THE RIVER'S TWISTS AND TURNS.

WHEN I THINK ABOUT THE CHAOS HE WROUGHT, IT'S ALMOST SAD TO SEE HIM HELD IN CHECK BY SOME VULGAR SAND MONSTER.

CAREFUL, SHASENG IS NO NEWCOMER. HE IS THE GENERAL OF THE ETERNAL WATERFALL, EXILED TO EARTH FOR A FAULT COMMITTED IN HEAVEN.

IN HER MAGNIFICENCE, THE BODHISATTVA AGAIN ACCEPTED TO HELP SUN WUKONG.

AH-HAH! ANOTHER STRAY!

SHE ENTRUSTED TO PRINCE HUI'AN THE MISSION OF GOING TO SUBDUE SHASENG.

AFTER ARRIVING AT THE RIVER, HUI'AN CALLED DO SHASENG BY HIS HEAVENLY TITLE OF GENERAL.

SHASENG SUBMITTED PEACEFULLY, FOR HE HAD BEEN CONVERTED TO THE GOOD BY THE BUDHISATTVA.

GUANYIN MADE SHASENG PROMISE TO AWAIT THE PASSAGE OF A MONK ON A QUEST FOR SUTRAS AND JOIN HIM.

BELIEVING HIMSELF TO BE UNDER ATTACK, THE MONK DIDN'T RECOGNIZE HIS MASTER!

PRINCE HUI'AN EXPLAINED THE MISUNDERSTANDING.

AH, LACK OF COMMUNICATION IS OFTEN THE ORIGIN OF TERRIBLE CONFLICTS.

OUR PILGRIMS FINALLY CROSSED THE RIVER AND RESUMED THEIR JOURNEY.

TELL ME MORE THOUSAND-LEAGUE EYE, I'M EAGER TO KNOW IT!

A NEW TRIAL AWAITED ZHU BAJIE, MAJESTY.

OUR PILGRIMS ARRIVED WHERE A RICH WIDOW AND HER THREE DAUGHTERS LIVED...

...AND THEY WERE EXPECTED.

I DARE NOT IMAGINE WHAT FOLLOWED...

HEIR TO THE UNIMAGINABLE FORTUNE OF HER HUSBAND, THE WIDOW WARMLY WELCOMED OUR PILGRIMS, CONCEALING NOTHING FROM THEM.

HEH! SOMETHING TO AROUSE VARIED APPETITES!

NOT ONLY THAT, MAJESTY, SHE OFFERED OUR MONKS NOTHING LESS THAN MARRIAGE!

A DAUGHTER FOR EACH DISCIPLE, AND THE WIDOW HERSELF TO XUANZANG...

...IN EXCHANGE FOR ABANDONING THEIR QUEST AND BREAKING THEIR VOW OF ABSTINENCE.

HA! I CAN JUST PICTURE THE FACE OF EACH OF OUR VOYAGERS!

XUANZANG COULDN'T EVEN IMAGINE ACCEPTING.

HE WAS FIRM IN HIS RESOLUTION, TO THE WIDOW'S GREAT DISPLEASURE.

REJECTED, SHE EJECTED THEM FROM HER HOME...

DID SHE SECRETLY HOPE THEY'D COME BACK THROUGH THE WINDOW?

ZHU BAJIE HAD NOT REMAINED INDIFFERENT TO THE WIDOW'S LOVELY OFFER.

THE PIG ATTEMPTED TO GIVE THEM THE SLIP WHILE THEY SLEPT. HE DIDN'T COUNT ON WUKONG'S PERCEPTIVENESS...

ZHU BAJIE OFFERED TO MARRY THE FOUR SUPERB WOMEN, INCLUDING THE MOTHER!

THAT RASCAL OF A PIG KNOWS NO OTHER LIMIT THAN THAT OF HIS EXPANSIVE UNDERBELLY!

REJECTING POLYGAMY, THE WIDOW OBLIGED HIM TO A GAME OF BLIND-MAN'S BLUFF TO DECIDE.

SO TAKEN BY THEIR OFFER OUR FRIEND DIDN'T UNDERSTAND THEY WERE MOCKING HIM.

THE NEXT DAY, UPON AWAKENING, SUN WUKONG TOLD HIS MASTER THE WHOLE STORY. THE DOMAIN AND ITS RICHES WERE AN ILLUSION!

THE WIDOW AND HER DAUGHTERS WERE GODS OF THE FOREST.

DESPITE HIS ALLEGIANCE TO XUANZANG, ZHU BAJIE HAD NOT YET SUCCEEDED IN FREEING HIMSELF FROM THE PENCHANTS THAT CAUSED HIS MISFORTUNES.

MAJESTY, LET ME TELL YOU THE REST OF THE ADVENTURES OF SUN WUKONG!

WHAT A TALE. AND THEN?

THEY RESUMED THEIR TRIP TO REACH—

GOOD WIND EARS, IT'S TOO BAD. YOU MISSED THE BEST PART.

HEE HEE HEE!

HEE HEE HEE!

HEE HEE HEE!

HA HA HA!

SUN WUKONG, DO YOU KNOW IF THERE'S STILL A LONG WAY TO THE PARADISE OF THE WEST?

KNOW THAT I COULD GO BACK AND FORTH SEVERAL DOZEN TIMES IN A DAY...

BUT EVEN IF YOU HAD A THOUSAND LIFETIMES YOU WOULDN'T REACH IT.

DON'T LISTEN TO THE LIES OF THAT INSOLENT MACAQUE, MASTER! HE IS ONLY SEEKING TO TROUBLE YOU.

THIS TABLET LOOKS TO BE TAOIST.

萬壽山福
五莊觀洞

WELCOME TO THE RESIDENCE OF THE GREAT IMMORTAL, NOBLE PILGRIMS.

-;MMMMH!;- IT SURE IS NICE TO BE WELCOMED LIKE KINGS!

ALMOST LIKE GODS...

;PFFFFT; THE MASTER DOESN'T WELCOME US IN PERSON AND SENDS US UNDERLINGS IN HIS PLACE!

AREN'T YOU ASHAMED OF INSULTING OUR HOSTS?

PLEASE EXCUSE WUKONG, REVEREND BONZES. MY DISCIPLE IS A CHAMPION AT PROVOCATION.

WILL WE HAVE THE HONOR OF MEETING YOUR MASTER?

HE'S NOT HERE.

HE DEPARTED THIS MORNING FOR THE PALACE OF THE JADE EMPEROR.

KNOWING YOU WOULD PASS BY OUR TEMPLE, HE TASKED US WITH WELCOMING YOU.

HE OFFERS YOU THESE TWO GINSENG FRUITS AS A WELCOME GIFT.

TWO NEWBORNS! WHAT A HORROR!

DON'T MISAPPREHEND THEIR APPEARANCE, MASTER! THESE ARE FRUITS!

THEY'RE OUR MOST PRECIOUS POSSESSION, FOR THEY CONFER IMMORTALITY UPON THE ONE WHO CONSUMES THEM.

NEVER WILL YOU SUCCEED IN MAKING ME BELIEVE THAT BABIES GROW ON TREEES!

I WILL AWAIT YOUR MASTER'S RETURN TO TELL HIM OF THE BAD JOKE YOU'VE PLAYED ON ME!

IF THESE KIDS ARE TELLING THE TRUTH, I'D LIKE TO TASTE THEIR FRUITS!

I HEARD TALK OF THEM WHEN I LIVED IN HEAVEN, BUT I'VE NEVER SEEN ANY BEFORE.

OUR MASTER IS A FOOL! LET ME HANDLE IT!

MASTER, THIS WHOLE MATTER HAS UPSET YOU. WHILE YOU'RE RESTING, THE THREE OF US WILL ATTEND TO UNLOADING OUR BAGGAGE FOR THE NIGHT.

THAT'S A GOOD IDEA, YOU HAVE MY PERMISSION.

TOMORROW WE WILL LEAVE THIS PLACE WHERE THEY PRACTICE CANNIBALISM!

I MISJUDGED THEM!

THEY ARE CAPABLE OF TAKING GOOD INITIATIVES...

IF WE SAVE THE FRUITS UNTIL OUR MASTER'S RETURN, THEY'LL HARDEN AND GO TO WASTE.

WELL, LET'S GOBBLE THEM!

SHH!

MMMH, THAT MONK IS TRULY STUPID. HE'S MISSING OUT!

YOU'RE RIGHT. IT'S VERY GOOD!

DID YOU REMEMBER TO PUT THE GOLDEN CANE BACK IN ITS PLACE AFTER PICKING THEM?

DON'T WORRY, I PUT IT AWAY AT THE FOOT OF THE TRUNK.

WAIT FOR ME HERE. I'LL BE FIVE MINUTES.

WOW, A DREAM COME TRUE!

WHAT I WAS LOOKING FOR!

GONE.

THE FRUIT WAS ABSORBED BY THE SOIL, GREAT SAGE.

YOU'RE THE LOCAL DIVINITY. YOU'RE THE ONE WHO STOLE MY FRUIT.

I'D NEVER COMMIT SUCH SACRILEGE!

THAT PRECIOUS FRUIT IS RESERVED FOR THE ELITE, FOR IT NEEDS 9,000 YEARS TO REACH MATURITY. WHOEVER EATS IT SHALL LIVE 47,000 YEARS.

BAH, I'VE BEEN IMMORTAL SINCE I ERASED MY NAME FROM THE BOOK OF THE DEAD. BUT....

I'M STILL A GOURMAND.

THE FRUIT IS CAPRICIOUS. ON CONTACT WITH METAL, IT FALLS. WITH WOOD, IT DRIES OUT. WITH WATER, IT--

THANKS, OLD MAN. I UNDERSTAND.

I WANT MORE! YOU GOING BACK?

YOU'RE PIGGING OUT TOO FAST! YOU WON'T EVEN GET THE TASTE!

HOLD ON, THAT'S NO COMMON BOWL OF RICE IT'S A PRIVILEGE TO HAVE JUST TASTED ONE!

THAT ANIMAL HAS SOME CHEEK! AFTER THE THEFT HE JUST COMMITTED, HE TAKES THE LIBERTY OF MORALIZING!

THAT IS NOTHING COMPARED TO WHAT HE DID AFTERWARDS!

THAT HARDLY SURPRISES ME.

ALAS FOR OUR PILGRIMS, THE TWO YOUNG BONZES QUICKLY SPOTTED THE THEFT. FURIOUS, THEY CAME TO DEMAND AN EXPLANATION FROM THE THIEVES AND THEIR MASTER.

THE MACAQUE, OUTRAGED BY THEIR INSULTS, PLOTTED TO GET REVENGE.

ON THEM? THAT'S REVERSING THE ROLES!

HE HURRIED TO THE GARDEN TO UPROOT THE TREE THEREIN.

WHAT A CATASTROPHE!

THE TREE AND THE FRUITS, ALL LOST!

WHEN THEY DISCOVERED THE DISASTER, THE TWO BONZES TOOK ACTION!

THEY LOCKED OUR PILGRIMS IN THE RECEPTION ROOM UNTIL THEIR MASTER'S RETURN.

A SIMPLE DOOR, HOWEVER, WASN'T ENOUGH OF AN OBSTACLE FOR THE TRAVELERS! ONCE NIGHT CAME, THEY ESCAPED.

I'M RATHER SURPRISED TO SEE XUANZANG AS AN ACCOMPLICE TO A YET UNPUNISHED CRIME!

WAIT. THE STORY DOESN'T END THERE, MAJESTY.

FLEEING LIKE THIEVES AFTER BRINGING DISORDER INTO THAT HOUSE!

HOW CAN WE ASPIRE TO FIND THE WAY IN THESE CONDITIONS?

IT'S YOUR FAULT, CURSED MONKEY! I WILL NEVER BE ABLE TO TRUST YOU AGAIN!

YOU OTHERS, ARE SCARCELY WORTH MORE!

¿PFFF!!¿

MASTER, THERE THEY ARE!

WHEN I RETURNED FROM MY TRIP, MY DISCIPLES TOLD ME OF THE CRIME YOU COMMITTED... UPROOTING MY GINSENG TREE! AN IRREPLACEABLE TREASURE!

THERE'S THE TRULY GUILTY ONE, MASTER.

HE'S THE ONE WHO UPROOTED THE GINSENG TREE!

WHAT RIGHT HAVE YOU TO ACCUSE ME WITHOUT PROOF, YOU TWO LITTLE SNOT-NOSES?!

UH... I'M SORRY... I... UH... IT WASN'T ME.

NOTHING MAKES ME ANGRIER!

SUN WUKONG, HAVE YOU GONE MAD?!

WHAT'S HAPPENING?

WHERE'D THAT STORM COME FROM?

MY DISCIPLES, DO SOMETHING!

SUN WUKONG, WHERE ARE YOU?

DON'T MOVE! YOU NEARLY BLINDED ME WITH YOUR RAKE!

WHAT'S HAPPENING? WHERE ARE WE?

MASTER, IS IT YOU?

FOR A PIG'S SAKE, HERE WE ARE STUCK IN A BAG LIKE COMMON POTATOES!

LET'S GO BACK AND DEAL WITH THEM.

THESE PILGRIMS BEHAVED LIKE BANDITS, UNWORTHY OF THE MISSION ENTRUSTED TO THEM. WE MUST PUNISH THEM FOR THE GINSENG TREE.

XUANZANG WILL BE PUNISHED FIRST!

DON'T EVEN THINK ABOUT IT!

I STOLE THE FRUIT AND UPROOTED YOUR TREE. I SHOULD BE PUNISHED FIRST.

THAT MACAQUE REASONS WELL. YOU'LL BE WHIPPED FIRST.

COMPARED TO THE PUNISHMENT I UNDERWENT IN HEAVEN BEING WHIPPED IS NOTHING!

MASTER, HOW MANY DO I INFLICT?

ONE BLOW FOR EACH FRUIT THAT'S LOST.

WHOM DO WE ATTEND TO NOW?

XUANZANG, TO PUNISH HIM FOR THE BAD EDUCATION HE HAS GIVEN!

...

YOU HAVE A SENSE OF DEVOTION, AT LEAST!

WELL, AGREED. YOU'LL RECEIVE THE PUNISHMENT IN HIS PLACE!

THANKS...

THANKS...

EVEN IF MY MASTER DIDN'T EDUCATE US WITH ENOUGH AUTHORITY, IT'S MY PLACE AS HIS DISCIPLE TO UNDERGO THE PUNISHMENT IN HIS STEAD.

NOW, GO PREPARE THE GREAT CAULDRON AND BRING OIL TO A BOIL IN IT.

WE'LL HAVE A FRYING WITH THE SCOUNDRELS!

GOOD NEWS. A NICE HOT BATH WILL RELAX ME!

MASTER, IT'S BUBBLING!

PERFECT! DUNK SUN WUKONG!

HE WEIGHS A TON!

HEAVE HO! HEAVE HO!

HEY, YOU OTHERS, COME HELP US!

OWW! OUCH!

THE MONKEY DECEIVED US!

WHERE IS HE HIDING?

THERE!

STEALING MY FRUITS AND UPROOTING MY GINSENG TREE WASN'T ENOUGH FOR YOU?

MUST YOU ALSO BREAK MY POTS?!

I HAD TO GO PEE, GREAT IMMORTAL. YOU'D HAVE SCOLDED ME FOR DIRTYING YOUR OIL BATH!

YOUR HUMOR WON'T SAVE YOUR MASTER!

MY CHILDREN, PREPARE A NEW CAULDRON FOR XUANZANG!

DON'T PUNISH HIM...

IF YOU WITH-DRAW I PROMISE TO REVIVE THE GINSENG TREE!

HOW WILL YOU ACCOMPLISH THAT MIRACLE?

THERE'S NOTHING SIMPLER...

SUN WUKONS HAD THREE DAYS TO FIND A SOLUTION.

HE FIRST MET THREE IMMORTALS WHO LIVE ON THE PENGLAI ISLANDS.

THEY WERE WILLING TO HELP, BUT KNEW OF NO SOLUTION.

HE LEFT FOR FANGHU ISLAND WHERE THE SUPREME SOVEREIGN'S RESIDENCE IS FOUND.

BUT HE, TOO, COULD DO NOTHING.

HE REACHED THE ISLAND OF YINGZHOU, THE LAND OF IMMORTALS WITH CHILDRENS' FACES.

THEY HAD DEALINGS WITH SUN WUKONG DURING THE CELESTIAL WARS AND REFUSED TO SPEAK TO HIM.

THE MONKEY FINALLY DECIDED TO RETURN AND PLEAD HIS CASE TO GUANYIN.

THE GODDESS MADE HIM ADMIT HIS FAULTS AND, AFTER REPRIMANDING HIM, SHE AGREED TO HELP.

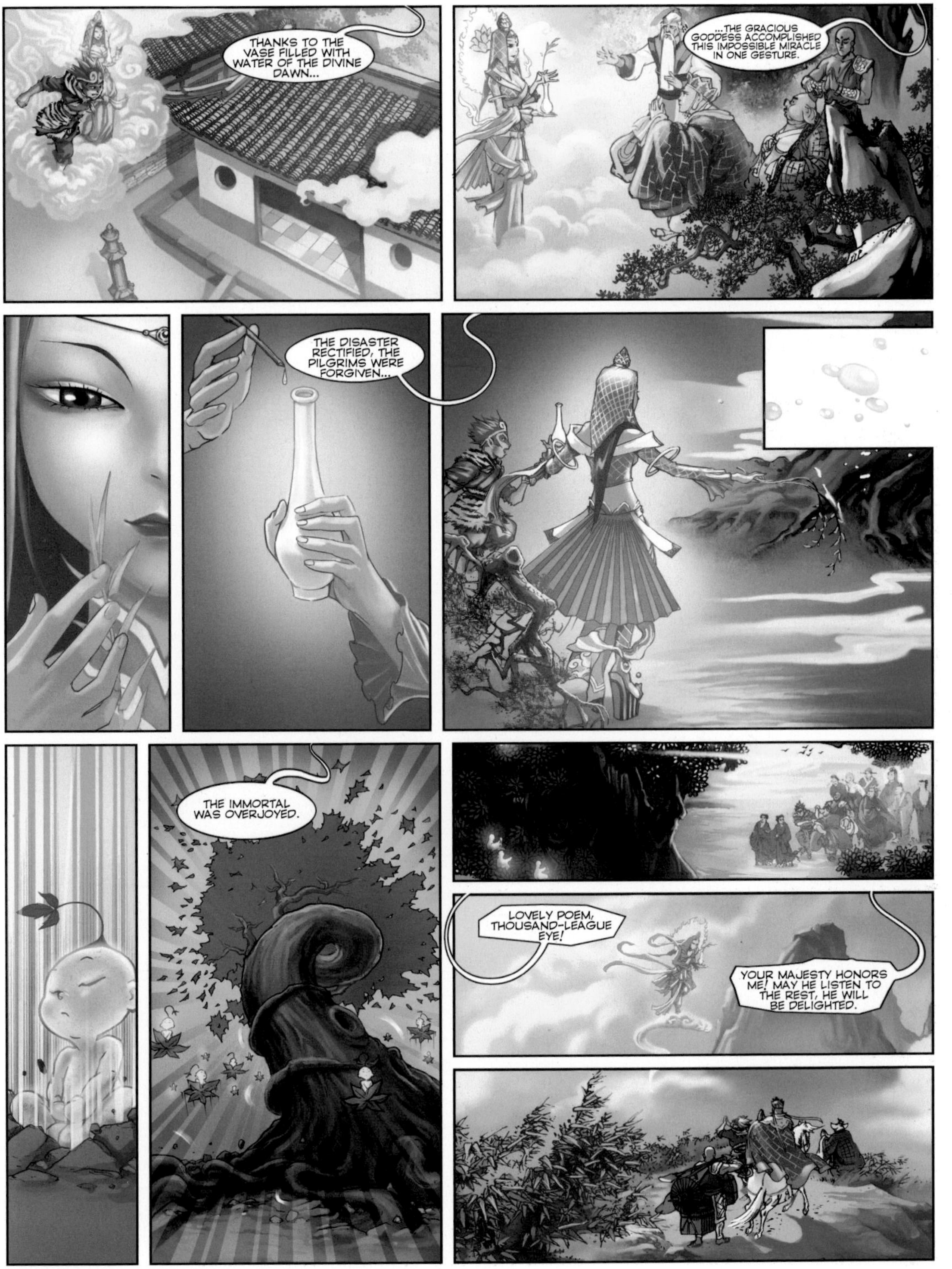
THANKS TO THE VASE FILLED WITH WATER OF THE DIVINE DAWN...
...THE GRACIOUS GODDESS ACCOMPLISHED THIS IMPOSSIBLE MIRACLE IN ONE GESTURE.
THE DISASTER RECTIFIED, THE PILGRIMS WERE FORGIVEN...
THE IMMORTAL WAS OVERJOYED.
LOVELY POEM, THOUSAND-LEAGUE EYE!
YOUR MAJESTY HONORS ME! MAY HE LISTEN TO THE REST, HE WILL BE DELIGHTED.

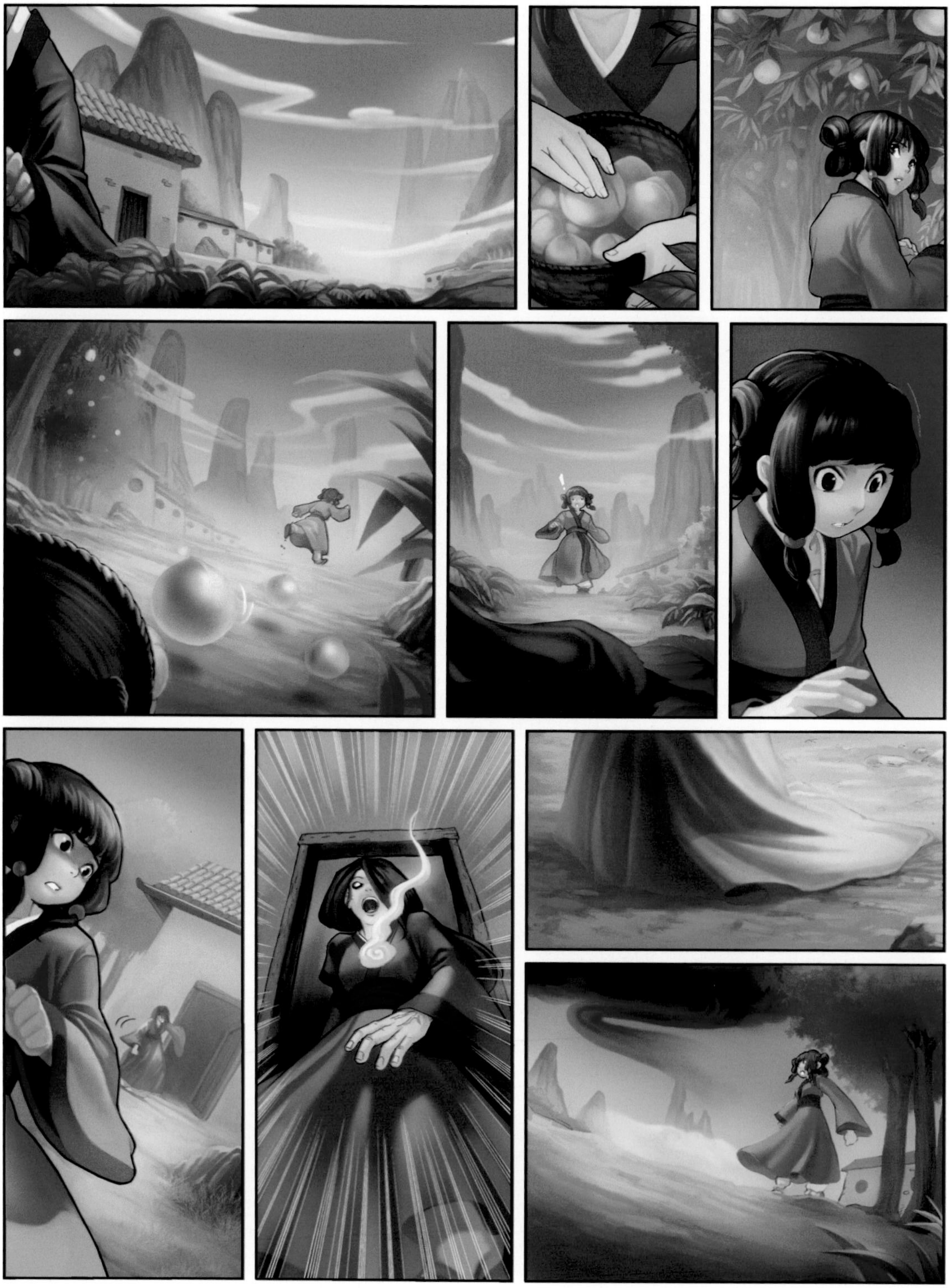

YOU SEEM RESTLESS, MASTER. BE REASSURED, SO LONG AS I'M AT YOUR SIDE, YOU'VE NOTHING TO FEAR.

...

THE ROAD HAS BEEN LONG. LET'S PAUSE FOR A BIT.

COOL! I'D SAY WE EACH DESERVE A REPOSE!

NOT SO FAST, SUN WUKONG! ABOVE ALL ELSE, I'M HUNGRY. GO FIND SOME LIGHT FOOD TO SUSTAIN ME!

BUT, MASTER, THOSE TWO IDIOTS ARE INCAPABLE OF PROTECTING YOU AGAINST THE THOUSAND DANGERS THAT LIE IN WAIT FOR YOU!

I PROPOSE TO WATCH OVER YOU WHILE THEY TRAIPSE ABOUT.

MY DISCIPLE, YOU STILL HAVE A LONG ROAD TO TRAVEL TO LEARN HUMILITY. MY DECISION IS MADE, AND IT'S YOU WHOM I ASKED.

I'LL GO, FOR I DON'T WANT YOU GOING AFTER MY HEAD AGAIN.

BUT TO BE CERTAIN NOTHING HAPPENS TO YOU IN MY ABSENCE, I'LL LEAVE YOU UNDER THE PROTECTION OF THIS MAGIC CIRCLE.

DON'T GO OUT BEFORE MY RETURN, OTHERWISE THE CHARM WILL BE BROKEN.

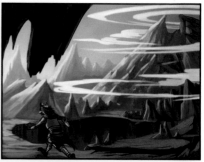

MISTRESS, I HAVE SOME NEWS THAT WILL DELIGHT YOU!

SOME FIRST-CLASS PREY ARRIVED IN YOUR LANDS TODAY! A MONK ON A MAGNIFICENT WHITE HORSE ACCOMPANIED BY A PIG, A TALL, ROBUST FELLOW, AND A CONCEITED MACAQUE.

XUANZANG, ZHU BAJIE, SHASENG AND-- SUN WUKONG!

THE MONKEY KING WHO DARED TO DEFY THE JADE EMPEROR IN PERSON! A TOUGH ADVERSARY, I'M NOT SURE I CAN VANQUISH HIM.

FOR THE MOMENT, HE HAS GONE TO FIND THEM FOOD.

SO, THEY'RE MOMENTARILY DEFENSELESS. IT'S NOW OR NEVER.

IF I DEVOUR THE MONK, I'LL GAIN IMMORTALITY!

BUT I'LL NEED A RUSE TO APPROACH THEM...

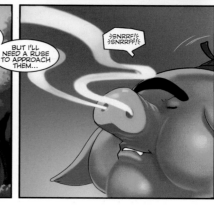

⸮SNRRF!⸮ ⸮SNRRFF!⸮

~MMMMHH!~ WHAT'S THAT LOVELY SMELL OF FOOD?

WELL, WELL, WELL! THAT'S A CHOICE PIECE COMING THIS WAY!

MISS!

SORRY?

FEAR NOT! I'M ONLY A HUMBLE MONK FROM THE EAST COME IN SEARCH OF SUTRAS!

AH!

?!

!

ZHU BAJIE, WHAT HAPPENED? WHO'S THAT YOUNG GIRL?

MASTER, I LIVE ON THE MOUNTAIN WITH MY PARENTS.

I WAS GOING TO THE TEMPLE OF THE DEVAS WHEN YOUR DISCIPLE HAILED ME.

WOULD YOU LIKE TO ACCOMPANY ME?

MASTER, WE'VE CROSSED NOT ONE SOUL OR TEMPLE IN THIS HOSTILE LAND. I THINK WE SHOULD AWAIT SUN WUKONG'S RETURN.

WHAT ARE YOU AFRAID OF, SHASENG? I SEE NO DEMON AROUND HER-- NOTHING BUT A YOUNG GIRL.

SHOW US THE WAY, MY CHILD. WE'LL FOLLOW YOU.

BEWARE, DEMON!

FEEL THE WEIGHT OF MY STAFF, IF IT'S TO YOUR LIKING!

ƷHRRF!Ƹ

WHAT ARE YOU ?!

... !

WAIT UP! DON'T THINK YOU'LL GET AWAY LIKE THAT!

HE'S NEVER BEEN VERY ENLIGHTENED, BUT THIS IS TERRIBLE!

AHHH!

CURSE HER!
I CAN'T SEE
NOW!

DARING TO TAKE A YOUNG GIRL'S LIFE! WHAT A CRIME!

AND I'D THOUGHT YOU WERE ON THE PATH TO REDEMPTION.

DAUGHTER! WHERE ARE YOU?

NOBLE MONKS, YOU HAVEN'T SEEN MY DAUGHTER, HAVE YOU?

I'M WORRIED. SHE LEFT TO BEAR SOME OFFERINGS TO THE TEMPLE, BUT SHE SHOULD BE BACK BY NOW.

AHH! MY DAUGHTER!

MY DAUGHTER-- DEAD! YOU PILGRIMS KILLED HER!

WE'RE RESPONSIBLE, BUT NOT GUILTY.

IT'S MY MONKEY WHO'S THE CAUSE OF ALL THIS UNHAPPINESS. HE FLED AFTER HIS CRIME.

YOU ARE ODIOUS, BARBARIC, CRUEL ASSASSINS! HOW COULD YOU KILL MY DAUGHTER LIKE THAT. SHE WAS ALWAYS WELL-BEHAVED AND OF GOOD VIRTUE, AND TOOK OFFERINGS TO THE BUDDHA!

I'M AT FAULT, I ADMIT IT. I HAVE FAILED IN MY TEACHING. MY DISCIPLES WILL ATTEND TO THE TOMB OF YOUR DEAR DECEASED.

I'LL SHOW YOU WHERE SHE WOULD HAVE LOVED FOR HER SOUL TO REST.

MY MASTER WON'T FOLLOW YOU ANYWHERE, DEMON!

SUN WUKONG?! BUT--

IT'S THE SAME DEMON AS IN THE GIRL! IT HAS CHANGED APPEARANCE AND IS GETTING READY TO POSSESS YOU.

WHAT IS THIS NOW?

AHHHH! HELP, THAT MONSTER IS THE DEVIL! SAVE ME.

MAYBE YOU CAN DECEIVE MY MASTER, BUT I CAN RECOGNIZE DEMONS.

THIS IS TOO EASY.

ANOTHER TRICK! IT GOT AWAY AGAIN!

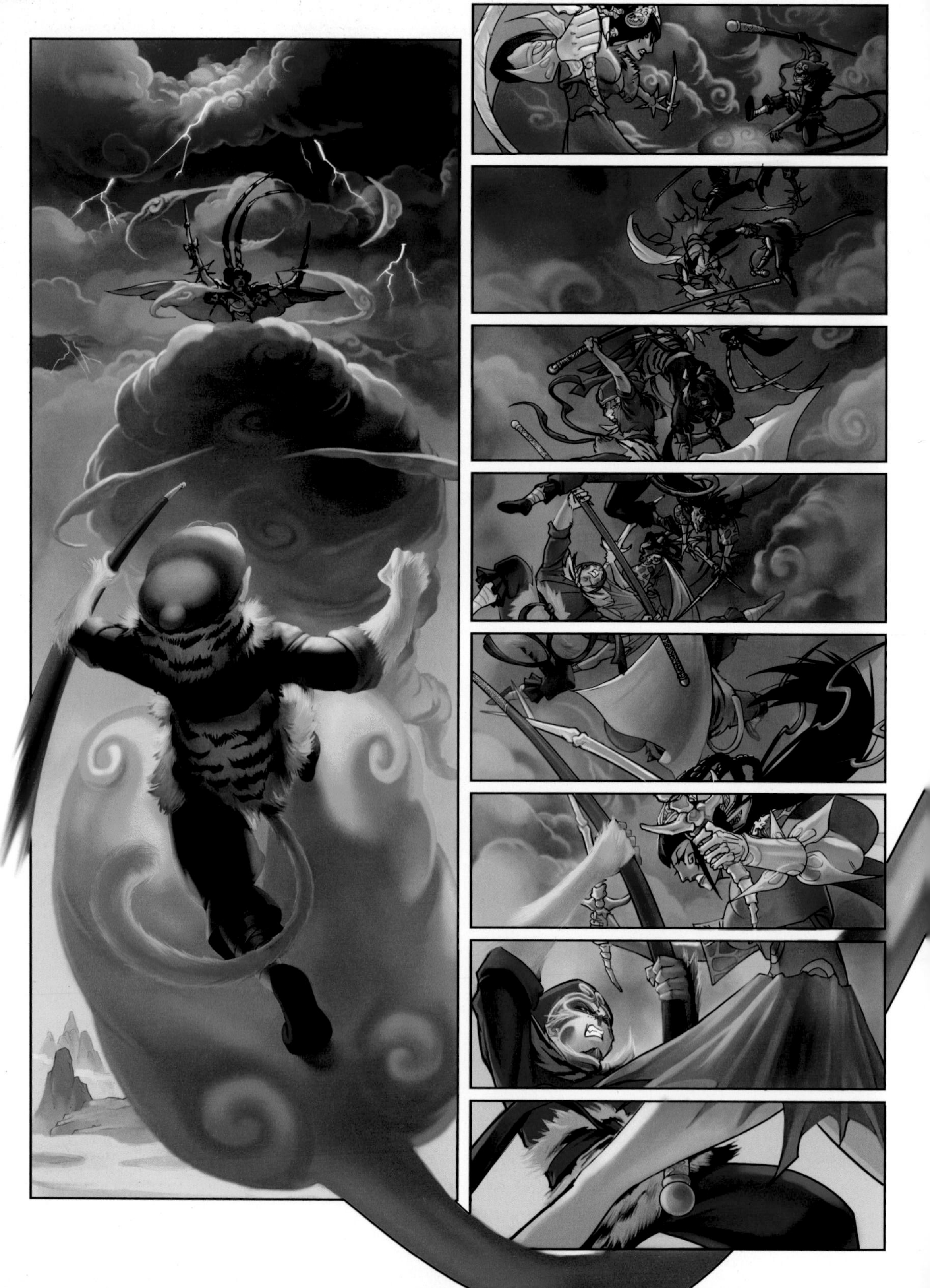

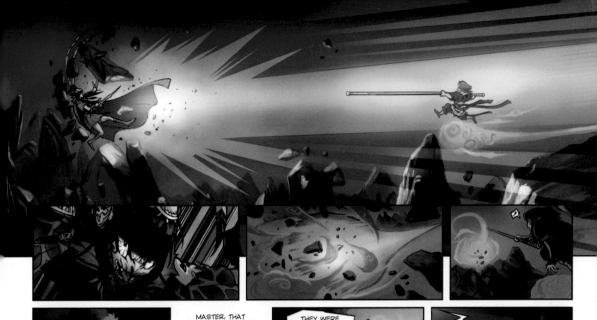

MASTER, THAT FALSE MOTHER AND DAUGHTER HAVE COMPLETELY DUPED YOU. THEY WERE DISGUISED DEMONS.

SUN WUKONG, YOU ARE A MONSTER! TAKING THE LIFE OF INNOCENT BEINGS IS A CRIME WHICH DISHONORS MY TEACHING!

THEY WERE DEFENSELESS CREATURES!

LET ME SHOW YOU YOUR ERROR.

YOU CAN SEE WHAT THE BASKET SUPPOSEDLY FILLED WITH APPETIZING FOOD CONCEALED.

HE MAY NOT BE WRONG, MASTER...

THOSE CREATURES ENTERED AFTERWARDS AND DEVOURED THE BASKET'S CONTENTS.

I'M TRULY WEARY OF YOU! I SEE NO OTHER RESPONSE TO YOUR BRUTALITY THAN THE BRUTALITY OF THE PUNISHMENT PRESCRIBED BY GUANYIN, OUR MISTRESS!

—ARGH!— I SWEAR I TOLD YOU THE TRUTH! THE DEMON FOOLED YOU.

STOP, MASTER, I BEG YOU! HE SAVED YOU! HE DOESN'T DESERVE SUCH SUFFERING. THINK ABOUT ALL THE TIMES HE SAVED YOUR LIFE!

SO BE IT! BUT KNOW THAT THE BUDDHA WILL JUDGE YOUR ACTS! AND JUSTICE WILL BE DONE.

WELL, YOUR JUSTICE ISN'T VERY JUST, MASTER.

MY, MY, WHAT A STORY, I SAY!

IN ANY CASE, EVEN THOUGH THE MACAQUE STILL HAS A WAYS TO GO TO LEARN HUMILITY, HE CANNOT BE REPROACHED FOR LACKING DEVOTION!

AS FOR XUANZANG, WE CAN'T SAY HE'S VERY PERCEPTIVE.

I SEE WHAT YOU MEAN, MILORD.

AND THE REST OF THE STORY WILL SHOW YOU HOW HE WILL BECOME THE VICTIM OF HIS OWN BLINDNESS.

TELL ME EVERYTHING. I'M VERY IMPATIENT TO KNOW WHAT FOLLOWS.

THE SKELETON WITCH WAS NOT DONE WITH OUR PILGRIMS, MAJESTY, AND WAS LAYING A NEW TRAP FOR THEM.

WHAT A CALAMITY, THIS EXPEDITION...

I'D TASKED YOU WITH FINDING FOOD, AND INSTEAD OF THAT, YOU'VE COMPROMISED ALL OF US.

APPEARANCES ARE BLINDING YOU.

THAT'S A NICE AROMA.

FEAST AND FAMINE ARE BEHIND THE DOOR!

SIR, WE'VE COME FROM THE EAST IN SEARCH OF SUTRAS. COULD YOU GRANT US ROOM? WE'LL PAY YOU, OF COURSE.

BE WELCOME. COME IN.

YOU MUST HAVE CROSSED MY WIFE AND DAUGHTER. THEY WERE GOING TO THE TEMPLE.

I'M WORRIED, FOR THEY SHOULD HAVE RETURNED LONG SINCE!

UH-- NO, WE'VE NOT SEEN ANYONE ON OUR JOURNEY.

BE CAREFUL, MASTER! THAT OLD MAN IS HIDING BENEATH HIS FEATURES THE DEMONESS!

THIS WHOLE FAMILY IS HER!

WHAT'S THE MONKEY TALKING ABOUT? IF YOU KNOW SOMETHING, TELL ME, I BESEECH YOU!

THEY'RE DEAD BENEATH THE BLOWS OF MY ROD.

AND YOU KNOW BETTER THAN I, YOU USURPED THEIR APPEARANCE!

DE-- DEAD? YOU KILLED THEM? THE ASSASSINS OF MY OWN FAMILY DARE TO COME TO MY HOME SEEKING HOSPITALITY?

UH, I-- IT'S NOT ME, IT'S HIM.

BE ON GUARD, MASTER, IT'S A RUSE.

HELP!

STOP THAT RAVING LUNATIC!

MASTER, WHAT IF SUN WUKONG'S RIGHT? HE'S SAVED OUR NECKS SEVERAL TIMES AND, WHEN IT COMES TO DEMONS, HE CAN RECOGNIZE THEM.

OF COURSE I'M RIGHT, YOU BIG SIMPLETON!

AS FOR YOU, I'LL FIND THE MEANS TO MAKE YOU APPEAR IN YOUR TRUE FORM!

STOP HIM BEFORE IT'S TOO LATE! OTHERWISE, YOU'LL HAVE MY DEATH TO ADD TO YOUR CONSCIENCE IN ADDITION TO THOSE OF MY WIFE AND CHILD!

UP THERE, LOOK!

?

"DESPITE ALL YOUR EFFORTS, SUN WUKONG HAS REMAINED PROUD AND UNCONTROLLABLE. HE CONTINUES TO BE A MURDERER, TOO.

"YOU MUST SEPARATE YOURSELF FROM HIM, OTHERWISE YOUR QUEST WILL NEVER SUCCEED."

AND IT'S SIGNED GUANYIN.

THE BODHISATTVA!

IMBECILES, YOU'LL ALL FALL INTO THE TRAP! BUT IT'S NO USE WITH ME, IT WON'T WORK.

AY YI YI! HELP, HELP ME!

SUN WUKONG, I ORDER YOU TO STOP!

SINCE THAT'S HOW IT IS, I SEE BUT ONE SOLUTION...

MASTER, WHY DO YOU TRUST THIS STRANGER MORE THAN YOUR SERVANT?

I'LL PROTECT YOU, DESPITE YOU!

CURSED MONKEY! I NEARLY SUCCEEDED THIS TIME, BUT I'LL HAVE MY REVENGE.

YOU'VE GONE TOO FAR, SUN WUKONG!

I CAN NO LONGER DO ANYTHING FOR YOU. I REFUSE TO ATTEMPT TO PURSUE YOUR EDUCATION, AND THIS WILL REMAIN THE GREATEST FAILURE OF MY LIFE.

YOU HAVE NOTHING FURTHER TO DO WITH US. RETURN TO YOUR MOUNTAIN AND REJOIN YOUR MONKEYS!

I DIDN'T SUCCEED IN PROVING THE DEMON'S PERFIDY TO YOU, BUT DON'T CHASE ME AWAY.

MANY DANGERS AWAIT YOU BEFORE YOU REACH THE SUTRAS, AND YOU'LL STILL HAVE NEED OF ME.

XUANZANG DIDN'T SEE IT THAT WAY. HE DIDN'T RECONSIDER.

SUN WUKONG GAVE HIS FINAL RECOMMENDATIONS TO ZHU BAJIE AND SHASENG SO THAT THEY COULD TAKE CARE OF THEIR MASTER, KNOWING THAT THEY FACED MANY DANGERS YET BEFORE ACHIEVING THEIR QUEST. THEN HE LEFT.

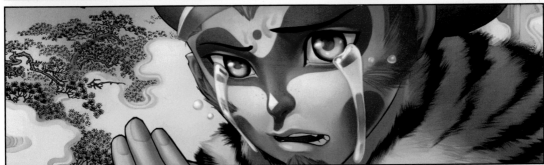

AFTER ALL THAT, WE STILL HAVEN'T EATEN. MY STOMACH'S RUMBLING.

LOOK OVER HERE!

THE TEMPLE OF THE DEVAS.

IT'S THE TEMPLE WHERE THE YOUNG PEASANT WHOM SUN WUKONG KILLED WAS GOING. SHE DIDN'T LIE-- THERE WAS NOTHING DEMONIC ABOUT HER!

LET'S GO BOW BEFORE THE STATUE OF THE BUDDHA TO PRAY FOR HER SPIRIT'S PEACE.

AND TO FIND SOME FOOD...

HA HA HA!

NOW YOU'RE CAUGHT IN THE TRAP, IMBECILIC MONK, INCAPABLE OF DISTINGUISHING THE TRUE FROM THE FALSE!

YOUNG MASTER, I'M GOING TO THE TEMPLE TO BEAR OFFERINGS TO THE BUDDHA. DO YOU WANT TO ACCOMPANY ME?

CURSED CRIMINALS! WHY DID YOU KILL MY DAUGHTER?

THANKS FOR SAVING MY LIFE BY PUNISHING AND CHASING AWAY SUN WUKONG!

THE MONKEY WAS RIGHT! I'VE BEEN THE PAWN OF A DEMON!

CAPTURE HIM!

I'M CAUGHT! ZHU BAJIE, SAVE XUANZANG!

TOO LATE! THE MASTER IS A PRISONER, TOO.

SAVE YOURSELF BEFORE YOU'RE CAUGHT, TOO!

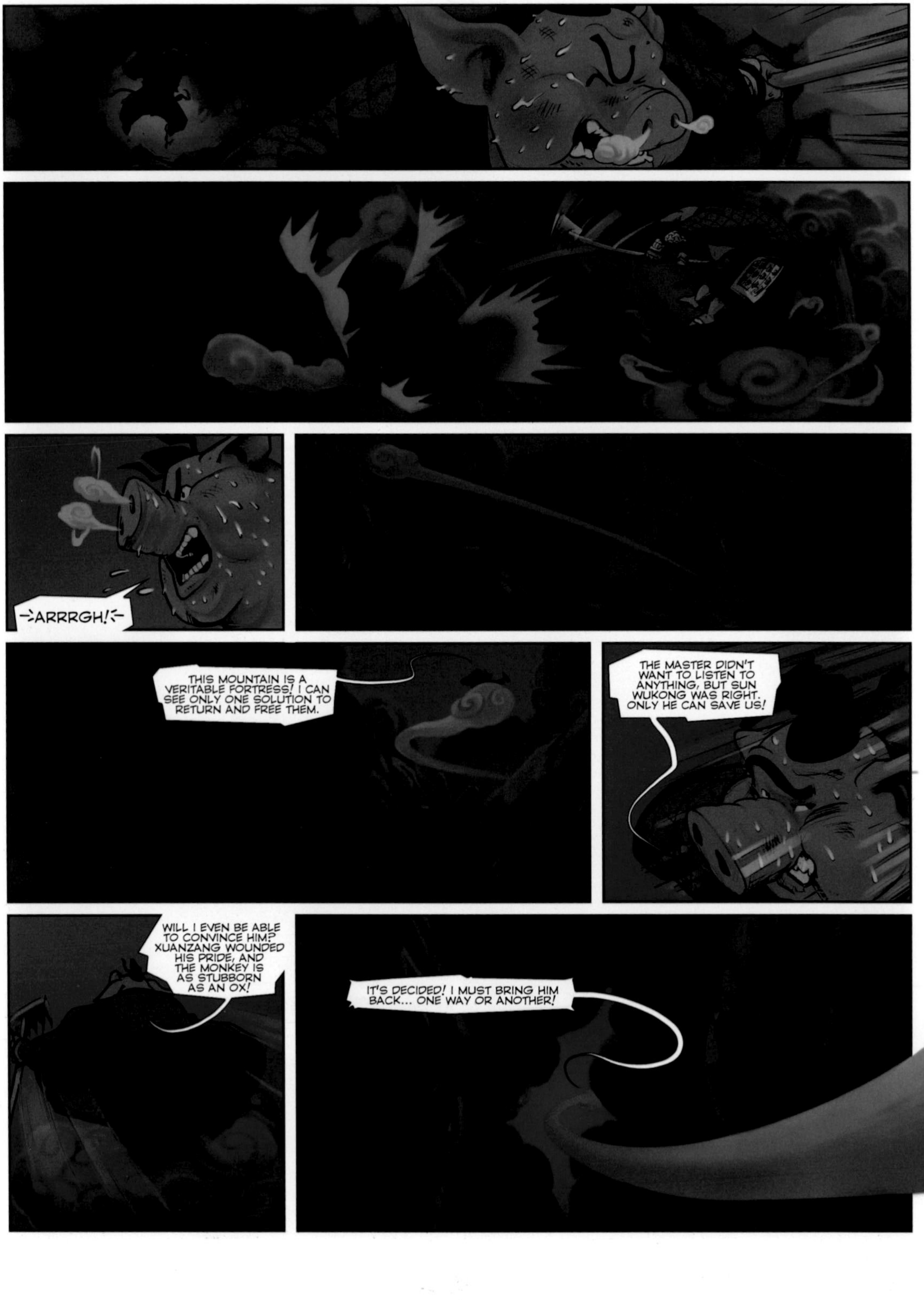

ARRRGH!
THIS MOUNTAIN IS A VERITABLE FORTRESS! I CAN SEE ONLY ONE SOLUTION TO RETURN AND FREE THEM.
THE MASTER DIDN'T WANT TO LISTEN TO ANYTHING, BUT SUN WUKONG WAS RIGHT. ONLY HE CAN SAVE US!
WILL I EVEN BE ABLE TO CONVINCE HIM? XUANZANG WOUNDED HIS PRIDE, AND THE MONKEY IS AS STUBBORN AS AN OX!
IT'S DECIDED! I MUST BRING HIM BACK... ONE WAY OR ANOTHER!

MOTHER, LET ME PRESENT TO YOU THE HIGH-RANKING GUESTS WE'RE HAVING TONIGHT FOR DINNER...

THE MONK XUANZANG, EN ROUTE TO THE WEST, IN SEARCH OF THE BUDDHA'S HOLY WRITINGS...

AND HIS DISCIPLE SHASENG!

THIS IMBECILIC PILGRIM FELL INTO MY TRAP. HE CHASED AWAY SUN WUKONG, HIS PROTECTOR.

BRAVO, MY CHILD!

I CAN'T WAIT TO FEAST ON THEIR DELICATE, SOUGHT AFTER FLESH.

TAKE THEM TO THE KITCHEN AND HAVE THEM ROASTED FOR US!

AND OVER A LOW HEAT, TOO, SO THEY DON'T DRY OUT.

THE GREAT SAGE, EQUAL OF HEAVEN!

GLORY TO HIS HOLINESS WHO FILLS US WITH HIS GIFTS!

GLORY! GLORY? GLORY?

~MMMMH~ IT'S GOOD TO BE THE KING!

HEY! WHO'S THAT?

?!?

GRAB HIM! DON'T LET HIM GET AWAY!

WELL, MY LITTLE SIMIANS, WHY ARE YOU DISTURBING THE PEACE OF THE CEREMONY?

IT'S NOT US, GREAT HOLINESS!

IT'S THIS STRANGER WHO SLIPPED AMONG US.

A BARBARIAN WITH A BIG SNOUT AND WHO SMELLS BAD.

BRING HIM TO ME!

I'M NOT A BARBARIAN AND I DON'T SMELL BAD! DON'T YOU RECOGNIZE ME?

ZHU BAJIE! HA HA HA! YOU'RE SO AFRAID OF ME THAT YOU HID BEHIND MY MONKEYS IN ORDER TO APPROACH ME?

BUT WHAT ARE YOU DOING HERE WHEN YOU SHOULD BE WITH XUANZANG. DID HE CHASE YOU AWAY, TOO?

NOT AT ALL.

THE MASTER... UH... THE MASTER MISSES YOU!

WHAT'S THIS? TRULY?

WELL, YES...THAT'S RIGHT...TRULY! AFTER YOUR DEPARTURE, HE BECAME UNHAPPY WITH OUR SERVICES.

HE STARTED SPEAKING ABOUT THE TIME WHEN YOU ACCOMPANIED US, ALWAYS QUICK TO COME TO HIS AID.

I'VE HEARD SOME GOOD ONES, BUT THAT ONE'S THE BEST!

PLEASE, DON'T MOCK ME! I'VE TRAVELED ALL THIS WAY TO COME FIND YOU.

I'M FLATTERED, SO LET YOURSELF HAVE A LITTLE FUN. YOU'RE MY GUEST.

UH, IT'S JUST THAT THE MASTER RISKS GROWING IMPATIENT. I MUSTN'T LINGER!

LET ME GIVE YOU A LOOK AROUND THE ESTATE, AT LEAST...

WOW! IT'S SO BEAUTIFUL.

WHEN I ARRIVED HERE, ALL WAS DESTROYED!

AFTER MY REBELLION IN HEAVEN, THE JADE EMPEROR WASN'T SATISFIED WITH BUDDHA'S PUNISHMENT

SO, HE SENT HIS ARMIES TO RANSACK MY DOMAIN.

WHEN I RETURNED, MY LITTLE MONKEYS HAD FLED OR WERE DEAD. ONLY A HANDFUL HAD REMAINED IN HOPES OF SEEING ME RETURN ONE DAY.

BUT THOSE SURVIVORS WERE UNDERGOING AN ORDEAL THEMSELVES, FALLING PREY TO CRUEL HUNTSMEN.

MY FIRST TASK, WAS TO ELIMINATE THOSE EVIL FOLKS.

THEN, I OCCUPIED MYSELF WITH RESTORING MY DOMAIN. I WENT TO PAY A VISIT TO THE DRAGON KING OF THE FOUR SEAS TO BORROW SOME IMMORTAL FRESH WATER FROM HIM.

WITH THE HELP OF MY MONKEYS, WE REFURBISHED EVERYTHING!

AND THAT'S HOW I REBUILT PARADISE BETTER THAN EVER!

THIS PLACE IS TRULY MAGNIFICENT!

AND HOW! WHEN I THINK THAT I WAS IDIOTIC ENOUGH TO WASTE MY TIME FOLLOWING XUANZANG ON HIS STUPID QUEST... I'M VERY HAPPY HE FINALLY DISMISSED ME.

YES, BUT AS I WAS TELLING YOU, HE MISSES YOU, AND HE'D LIKE YOU TO COME BACK FOR A LITTLE WHILE.

YOU CAN'T TEACH AN IMMORTAL MONKEY NEW TRICKS. I VERY MUCH DOUBT THAT THE MONK MISSES ME, BUT HE MUST BE IN DANGER, AND THAT'S WHY YOU'VE COME IN SEARCH OF ME.

XUANZANG FELL INTO A TRAP AND IS THE PRISONER OF THE SKELETON WITCH! IF YOU DON'T COME RIGHT AWAY, SHE AND HER MONSTERS WILL DEVOUR HIM!

THERE WE ARE! THE MONK WAS HAD! ALL THAT WOULDN'T HAVE HAPPENED IF HE'D LISTENED TO ME.

AGREED, BUT ENOUGH WASTING TIME WITH CHATTER. TIME IS PRESSING AND WE MUST GO NOW!

NOT SO FAST, MY FRIEND!

WHY WOULD THE MONKEY KING GO TO SAVE THAT MONK'S SKIN, WHO TREATED HIM LIKE A NOBODY, AND CAN'T EVEN TELL TRUE FROM FALSE?!

YOU'RE NOTHING BUT AN OLD, CONCEITED, UNGRATEFUL MACAQUE! DON'T FORGET THAT HE'S THE ONE WHO FREED YOU FROM ETERNAL IMPRISONMENT.

AND ON THAT DAY, HE DID AN EXTREMELY GOOD DEED! BUT THAT CHANGES NOTHING-- THE MONKEY KING REMAINS IN HIS DOMAIN.

NOW THAT YOU HAVE READ THE CLASSICS Illustrated EDITION, DON'T MISS THE ADDED ENJOYMENT OF READING THE ORIGINAL OBTAINABLE AT YOUR SCHOOL OR PUBLIC LIBRARY.

WATCH OUT FOR PAPERCUTZ™

Welcome to the thrilling, twelfth CLASSICS ILLUSTRATED DELUXE, from Papercutz, the company dedicated to publishing great graphic novels for all ages. I'm Jim Salicrup, the monkey-brained Editor-in-Chief and Keeper-of-the-Banana-Treats.

In past CLASSICS ILLUSTRATED DELUXE graphic novels we've mainly featured adaptations of stories that have been adapted into comics in CLASSICS ILLUSTRATED before—stories such as Frankenstein or The Three Musketeers—but in new longer, more faithful form. This time around we're trying something a little different. We're adapting a Chinese myth, that's influenced everything from Akira Toriyama's super-successful manga series Dragon Ball Z (the main character, Son Goku, is based on Sun Wukong) to Jamie Hewlett and Damon Albarn's musical, "Monkey: Journey to the West." (The BBC later commissioned Hewlett and Albarn to create a two-minute animated film, using the "Monkey" characters playing in various sports, to help promote their coverage of the 2008 Olympics in Beijing. Which appeals to us a lot, because we also published THE SMURFS #11 "The Smurfs Olympics" and GERONIMO STILTON #10 "Geronimo Stilton Saves the Olympics," so we love seeing animated characters compete!)

While in previous volumes we have tried different things such as presenting a manga-style adaptation of "The Adventures of Tom Sawyer" in CLASSICS ILLUSTRATED DELUXE #4, and adapting the lesser-known Dickens tale, "A Remembrance of Mugby," and presenting it along with an adaptation of "A Christmas Carol" in CLASSICS ILLUSTRATED DELUXE #9, "The Monkey God" is something completely different compared to what we've been publishing up until now

As Jean David Morvan (who has scripted the adaptations for CLASSICS ILLUSTRATED DELUXE #4, 6, and 10), explains in his introduction, "The Monkey God" is based on one of the "four pillars of Chinese literature." Unlike the American and English novels and short stories we've been presenting in CLASSICS ILLUSTRATED DELUXE up til now, this is a tale steeped in a very foreign culture. But we believe that for CLASSICS ILLUSTRATED DELUXE to remain viable, we need to try to bring you stories you may not have encountered before, while not abandoning the tradition of "featuring stories by the world's greatest authors."

Speaking of which, there's even debate about the authorship of "The Monkey God." Historians believe Wu Cheng'en did indeed write a book called "The Journey West," but are now uncertain if it was this story. But since he has been attributed as the author for so long, and there are scholars who believe he is still the one most likely to have written it, we'll keep his name on it too.

Over the years there have been many English translations, providing very different takes on the story. While, 1942's *Monkey: A Folk Tale of China,"* an abridged translation by Arthur Waley was popular for a very long time, a more faithful complete adaptation by Anthony C. Yu, entitled *"The Journey to the West,"* was published in four volumes, from 1977-1983.

At the end of many CLASSICS ILLUSTRATED adaptations, there's usually a caption that advises: Now that you have read the CLASSICS ILLUSTRATED edition, don't miss the added enjoyment of reading the original, obtainable at your school or Public Library. In regards to "The Monkey God," that's an understatement! As Editor Michael Petranek explains...

Journey to the West is a massive work, and adapting the entire novel into comics would take hundreds upon hundreds of pages. This adaptation consists of mainly the first 30 chapters out of 100(!). I sincerely suggest picking up the novel to continue the voyage of Sun Wukong. It's an epic quest with a lot of similarities to J.R.R. Tolkien's *The Lord of the Rings* trilogy, though it was written over 300 years prior. The novel's definitely worth seeking out, as this adaptation just gives a hint of the wonders that await you.

Stay in Touch!

EMAIL: salicrup@papercutz.com
WEB: papercutz.com
TWITTER: @papercutzgn
FACEBOOK: PAPERCUTZGRAPHICNOVELS
FAN MAIL: Papercutz, 160 Broadway, Suite 700,
            East Wing, New York, NY 10038

Let us know what you think of "The Monkey God," as we've got some even wilder upcoming adaptations we're hoping to spring on you in upcoming editions of CLASSICS ILLUSTRATED DELUXE!

Thanks, Jim

AN APOLOGY: In CLASSICS ILLUSTRATED DELUXE #11 "The Sea-Wolf" by Jack London, adapted by Riff Reb's, we altered the ending of Riff Reb's adaptation to be closer to the original ending by Jack London. We meant no disrespect to Riff Reb's, and in the event of future printings of CLASSICS ILLUSTRATED DELUXE #11 "The Sea-Wolf" we will restore Riff Reb's ending. We apologize to Riff Reb's, who created an awesome adaption, for our mistake in judgment.

Special Preview of CLASSICS ILLUSTRATED #19 "The Adventures of Tom Sawyer"

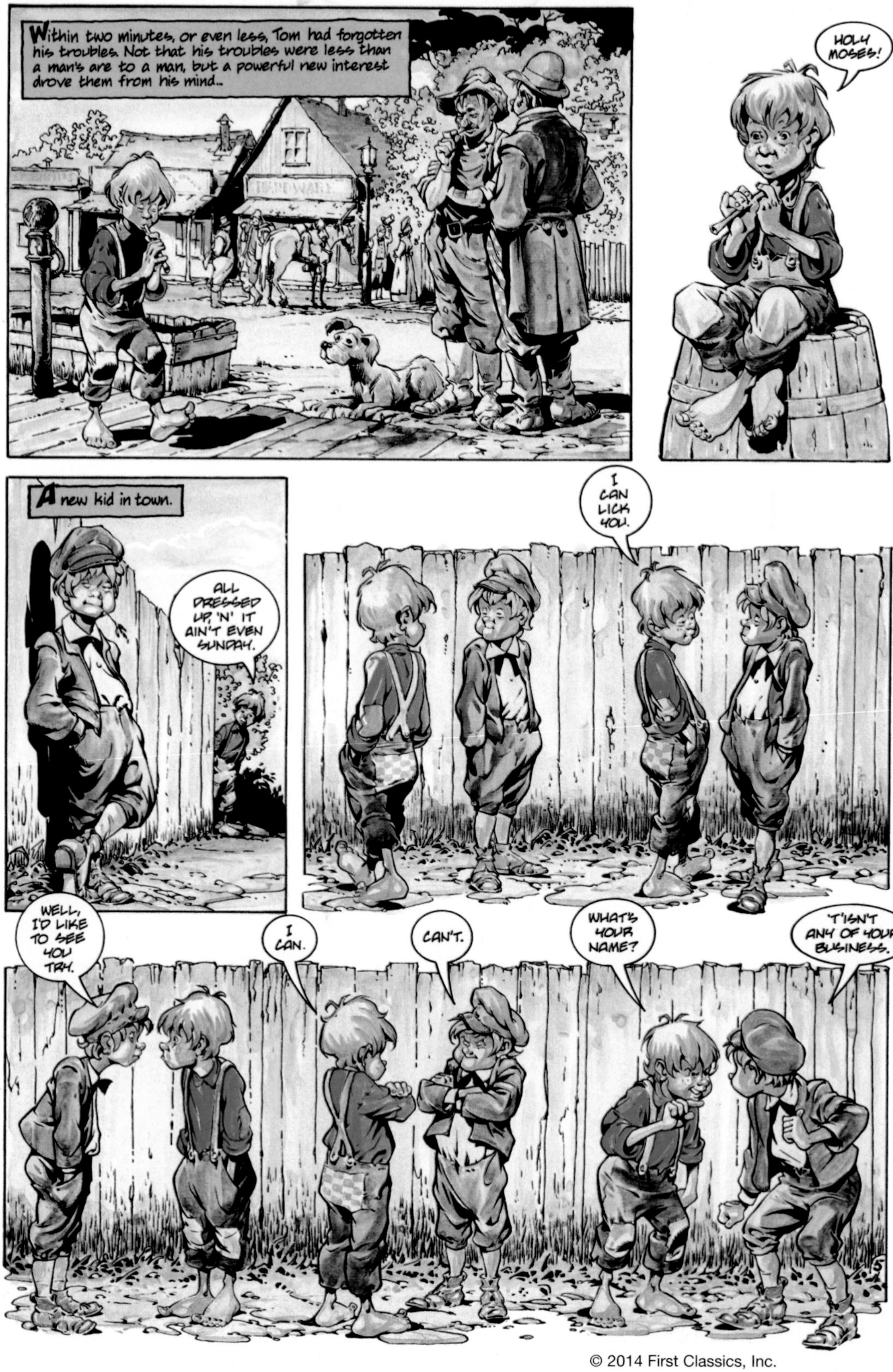
Within two minutes, or even less, Tom had forgotten his troubles. Not that his troubles were less than a man's are to a man, but a powerful new interest drove them from his mind...
HARDWARE
HOLY MOSES!
A new kid in town.
ALL DRESSED UP, 'N' IT AIN'T EVEN SUNDAY.
I CAN LICK YOU.
WELL, I'D LIKE TO SEE YOU TRY.
I CAN.
CAN'T.
WHAT'S YOUR NAME?
'T'ISN'T ANY OF YOUR BUSINESS.
5

Don't Miss CLASSICS ILLUSTRATED #19 "The Adventures of Tom Sawyer"

CLASSICS ILLUSTRATED GRAPHIC NOVELS
AVAILABLE FROM PAPERCUTZ

#1 "GREAT EXPECTATIONS"

#2 "THE INVISIBLE MAN"

#3 "THROUGH THE LOOKING-GLASS"

#4 "THE RAVEN AND OTHER POEMS"

#5 "HAMLET"

#6 "THE SCARLET LETTER"

#7 "DR. JEKYLL & MR. HYDE"

#8 "THE COUNT OF MONTE CRISTO"

#9 "THE JUNGLE"

#10 "CYRANO DE BERGERAC"

#11 "THE DEVIL'S DICTIONARY AND OTHER WORKS"

#12 "THE ISLAND OF DOCTOR MOREAU"

#13 "IVANHOE"

#14 "WUTHERING HEIGHTS"

#15 "THE CALL OF THE WILD"

#16 "KIDNAPPED"

#17 "THE SECRET AGENT"

#18 "AESOP'S FABLES"

COMING SOON:

#19 "THE ADVENTURES OF TOM SAWYER"

#20 "THE FALL OF TH HOUSE OF USHER"